MW00938695

Expanded Praise for *The Grandma Gang*

"Popular culture, including books that resonate deeply with the reader, can change attitudes and remove stigma surrounding people with disabilities. Stigma has held back the inclusion of people with disabilities in our society. While people with disabilities are twenty percent of the world's population, they are routinely ostracized from our places of work, culture, housing and education. This trend must stop. I believe that changing public attitudes will do more to bring equality to people with disabilities than any piece of legislation. *Mary Grace and the Grandma Gang* is joining a growing trend of books, movies and tv shows to accurately portray people with disabilities. I highly recommend it."

—Jay Ruderman,
President of the Ruderman Family Foundation

A Grandma Gang Mystery

Donny and Mary Grace's California Adventures

VOLUME I

Catherine Anna Pepe

Published by Redwood Publishing, LLC
Orange County, CA
info@redwooddigitalpublishing.com

First Printing, 2021

ISBN 978-1-956470-11-6 (paperback)
ISBN 978-1-956470-12-3 (e-book)

Library of Congress Control Number: 2021918786

Cover and Interior Illustrations: Redwood Publishing, LLC
Interior Design: Jose Pepito

Disclaimer: This is a work of fiction. Names, characters, places, and incidents either are the product of the author's imagination or are used fictitiously. Any resemblance to actual persons, living or dead, events, or locales is entirely coincidental.

Visit www.grandmagangmysteries.com for more information on the Grandma Gang series.

10 9 8 7 6 5 4 3 2 1

Please note that 10 percent of the net proceeds from the sales of this book will be donated to the Special Olympics.

DEDICATION

This book is dedicated with love to
Donald Woodward Burcham
March 4, 1955 – July 20, 2008

Your life made our lives better.

Thank you,
Cathy, Mary, and David

AUTHOR'S NOTE

I was fourteen years old in 1955, when my brother Donny was born. Yes, there is a real Donny!

My dad took me out to lunch the day after his birth to tell me that I had a new baby brother, and that the doctors said he had Down syndrome. I had never heard of Down syndrome and asked my dad what that meant. He said that Donny would have some special problems, that he might not live very long, and that if he did live, his life would be different from the lives of my sister, my brother, and me. He told me the doctors said he would never be normal, go to normal schools like other kids, and might never learn how to walk, talk, read, use the bathroom, or otherwise have a "normal" life. With tears in his eyes, he said that the doctors recommended that he and my mother put Donny into an institution or a special home for what was left of his life.

By then we were both crying. My father hugged me and then told me the most surprising thing of all: he and my mother had decided they would keep Donny at home, and that we would love him and help him learn everything he could. I smiled then and promised that we would all help Donny have a good life, whatever that meant.

That day was the start of a marvelous adventure, one in which Donny changed our lives for the better and taught us that all human life is special and offers special benefits. Donny was fortunate to be born at a time when medical science was doing amazing things with miraculous drugs. Donny lived until he was fifty-three years old; learned to walk, talk, read, sign greeting cards, use the bathroom, play the church's organ with foot pedals; and fell in love with American history.

By the time he was ten, he could name all the presidents and their wives, where they were born, and where they were buried. He loved life, his family, and his series of dogs. Every morning when he woke up, he would shout, "Today is the best day of my life!"

Before Donny came into our lives, the best way to describe our parents' first three children was "dedicated over-achievers." My sister, Mary, went back to college with three children under the age of five at home and became a certified public accountant—passing the multipart exam on her first try—and ultimately became the co-owner of a respected accounting firm in Silicon Valley, where she worked until her retirement last year. Our other brother, Dave, went back to school with young children at home, finished the course work for his PhD, and then went to law school. He was chosen to be a clerk for Justice Byron White on the US Supreme Court, and then became the dean of Loyola Law School and, ultimately, the first and only non-Jesuit president of Loyola Marymount University in Los Angeles, where he worked until retirement.

I went to law school after staying home with two sons for eleven years, and graduated summa cum laude (as did Dave)—but I was number *two* in the class of four hundred. I paid for law school tuition (then much less than today) by winning two TV game shows. I ultimately went to work for an international law firm and became the first woman partner in the labor and employment law practice group, where I worked until retirement.

I wrote the first drafts of the first three Mary Grace and Donny books during the pandemic, after I got bored with watching daytime TV and doing needlepoint. These books are clearly fiction, but some of the characters and incidents were inspired by living with Donny and the rest of my amazing family. I hope you too, will shout with Donny, "Today is the best day of my life!"

ACKNOWLEDGMENTS

I gratefully acknowledge a number of special people who helped me with this book. First, my Editor Michael Levin who is the most patient and thorough teacher—he taught me things about writing I never learned in school. Second, my husband Steve Pepe, who is probably the best proofreader I've ever worked with, even though he has "staff" in his real job who proofread for him. Next, my college roommate Caroline Willsie (Occidental College, 1964) who lived in Wichita and researched all the information about the zoo and the park, and who read every word of every draft—many times—and made many excellent suggestions. And honorable mentions to Francesca Lindley, who spent the afternoon in our backyard with us both wearing masks during the Covid pandemic, rewriting awkward passages; Father Randall Day and his husband Billy Hurbaugh, who really don't like tuna casserole or red jello, but who have been to more church suppers than anyone I know; Nichole Dechaine and her sons Michael and William, who stayed up past their bedtime to read one of the earlier drafts so they could find out what happened to Justin; My sister Mary Blythe and her granddaughter Penelope who really does speak Mandarin; my brother and wife Dave and Chris Burcham, who provided technical legal help (Dave, a retired law school professor and dean) and story structure help (Chris, a retired children's librarian); my daughter-in-law Krista Ruetz Hagen, who has taught Down syndrome and other special needs children for many years, and Steve Claypool, a retired teacher and good friend who used the "suggestion" box in his own classroom for help with classroom dramas and mysteries.

CHAPTER

ONE

The loudspeakers, perched high on poles and trees at the Sedgwick County Zoo in Wichita, Kansas, crackled and came booming to life: "Attention, please. A five-year-old boy is lost somewhere in the zoo. His name is Donny Miller. Donny is wearing a brand-new, bright-blue Sedgwick County Zoo T-shirt. Please help us find Donny. If you see Donny, please bring him to the nearest zoo ranger or information station . . . or to the zoo's entrance. Tell Donny that his parents are there and cannot wait to see him. Let's all keep an eye out for Donny and help him get back to his parents! Thank you for your help. And Donny, if you're hearing this—don't worry! We will get to you soon; keep your eyes peeled for a ranger, and tell them who you are. They'll be sure to wait with you!"

Ten-year-old Mary Grace Miller was just leaving the penguin exhibit when she heard the announcement about Donny. She immediately started running. Donny was her brother, and he had Down syndrome. She had been with him and their parents less than ten minutes earlier. They had been on their way out of the zoo when Mary Grace realized that Donny's favorite blanket was missing. "He must have left it at the penguin exhibit! Wait here," she said, and ran off to find the blanket. He had been standing right next to their parents when she left.

Had he wandered off? she wondered. *Was he in danger? Did someone take him?* Mary Grace's mind was racing as she made her way back toward the zoo's entrance with the blanket—which had been right by the penguin pool, just as she'd figured. She was glad she was wearing her new Nikes. She felt as if they made her run faster. She sped up as she rounded the final corner and saw her parents, John and Jen Miller, at the gate. Her father was pacing back and forth in front of the gate, and her mother was talking to some man, probably somebody who worked at the zoo. Her parents were both very outgoing, but her dad was more of a deep thinker, and her mom was more of an extrovert, always talking and asking questions.

"What happened?" Mary Grace asked them, breathing hard from her run. "Where's Donny? Which way did he go?"

"I don't know," said her mom. "One minute, he was here, and the next minute, he was gone! I should have been watching him more closely."

Mary Grace could see tears in her mom's eyes and hear a little guilt in her voice. She didn't want to make her parents more upset than they already were; they felt bad enough already. She understood that her parents had devoted their lives to their kids and wanted to give her brother the best life a kid could have. They were the last people who should ever feel guilty.

"Don't worry, Mom. Stuff like this happens all the time," she said in her calmest voice. We'll find Donny. He couldn't have gone far."

But her mom *was* worried. Mrs. Miller knew that a zoo was not the safest place for a lost boy.

"Maybe Donny decided to check out some of the exhibits we missed," she said, "or went to find a bathroom." In her mind, she was thinking about worse things: *What if he'd tried to get into the alligator pond or was in some other kind of danger?*

Mr. Miller suddenly stopped pacing. He seemed to be deep in thought, but he had heard every word of the conversation. As always, he and Mrs. Miller were in sync, and it was almost as if he'd heard her thoughts as he was deep in his. *Oh no! The snake exhibit,* he'd thought, *or worse… alligators!* Without saying a word, he quickly took off to his left and headed in the direction of the alligator pond.

"Stay here, Mom, in case he comes back," said Mary Grace before she, too, dashed off. She was headed to the monkey exhibit.

When she arrived, the monkeys were putting on a good show—scratching, screeching, eating, and throwing food at the windows—and the crowd was loving it. Mary Grace waited for a pause in the action before speaking up.

"Attention, everybody," she said, and the crowd near the large window quieted down. "Have any of you seen my brother, Donny? He's five years old and wearing a bright-blue T-shirt."

The crowd gave her only blank stares and sympathetic looks. She put her head down and started to leave. Two long-haired teens suddenly stepped in front of her.

"We'll help you find your brother!"

"Wow, thanks!" said Mary Grace. Nobody had seen Donny, but these two teenage boys were saying they would help look for him. Mary Grace was touched by the kindness of these most unlikely strangers. They looked like they would be the last people to offer their help, like kids who would be more interested in searching for trouble than for a little boy, but as Mom always said, *You can't judge a book by its cover.* As the sister of someone who looked a little different, she should know better.

"Where should we start?" one of the boys asked. "What do you want us to do?"

"I don't know. Donny was at the zoo's entrance ten or fifteen minutes ago, so he could be anywhere by now."

One of the boys took control: "Okay. Let's make a quick plan. We'll go around the zoo clockwise, stopping at each exhibit, looking and talking to people. You do the same thing going counterclockwise, and we'll meet up at the zoo's entrance in about ten minutes. We will ask anybody and everybody we come across if they have seen Donny."

"Don't worry," the second boy assured Mary Grace. "We'll find him. Donny. Bright-blue zoo T-shirt. We got this!"

Mary Grace smiled for the first time since the announcement over the loudspeakers. She thanked the boys over and over, and as she headed off, she could hear them yelling, "Donn-neee" as they went the other way.

Mary Grace headed in the opposite direction and made a quick counterclockwise loop through the zoo, but no one had seen her brother. How frustrating! As she headed dejectedly back toward the exit gate, she was still trying to figure out where Donny could be. She immediately noticed that her dad was back at the gate, pacing again and looking glum.

"Well, Donny wasn't at the alligator pond," he said, "or anywhere else I looked."

"It's a relief about the alligators, I guess," Mrs. Miller said, and gave Mary Grace a little smile.

Two men from the zoo staff had joined them.

One of them said, "We have asked the workers at all of the exhibits to carefully watch all crowd activity. And we are searching high and low for him all over the zoo. This is not the first time one of our young visitors has gotten lost—but we have found every one of them and gotten them right back to their families! I'm sure this adventure will also have a happy ending."

The two teenage boys joined the group at the gate.

"Any good news?" one of them asked.

"Not yet," said Mary Grace sadly.

After hearing that Donny was still missing, one of the boys pulled out his cell phone and posted messages to Facebook and Instagram, asking his friends and family at the zoo to help look for Donny.

"Hey," one of the boys said, turning to Mary Grace, "do you have a picture of your brother? I could add it to the post." He flashed his phone at her to show what he had written on Facebook.

Mary Grace quickly turned to her father.

"Dad, could you please find the pictures you took earlier, when Donny and I were walking and dancing like penguins?"

She watched as he swiped through the recent pictures in his phone.

"Stop," she said, pointing. "That one. That's it!" Then she laughed and shouted, "I think I know where Donny is!"

The zoo officials came over to look at the picture, as did the boys.

Mary Grace pointed at the photograph and explained what she'd noticed: "It's a picture of Donny and me standing right *here*, pretending to be penguins—but look in the background. There is a tram in the picture . . . but it's not here now! I bet Donny is on that tram! It looks like a train, and Donny loves trains."

Mary Grace asked her father when the picture was taken. He checked and said it had been taken exactly twenty-seven minutes earlier.

"I think we should check that tram," she said with a big grin.

The zoo official pulled out his walkie-talkie. He asked the tram operator to check if Donny was on the tram. He described Donny, then listened silently for a few long moments before a big smile suddenly appeared on his face.

"Good news!" he said. "Donny is on the tram. He was asleep on the very back seat, but he's awake now and happy. The tram is stopped near the giraffes for the moment, but the driver is going to head right back here."

Just a few minutes later, everyone watched and clapped as the tram approached the gate. They could see Donny sitting right up front with the driver. He had a big engineer's hat on his head and an even bigger smile on his face. He pulled the chain that blew the whistle three times. When the tram stopped, Donny gave the driver a high five and jumped off. He ran straight to his parents and Mary Grace, who had lots of hugs for him, but lots of questions too.

"My legs and arms were tired from walking and dancing like a penguin," Donny said, talking quickly because he was excited. "I didn't see Mary Grace, so I walked to the train to sit down. I guess I fell asleep, and the train started to go! Sorrrry." Then he shrugged and smiled.

Mary Grace could never be mad at Donny—at least not for long. She hugged him again and grabbed his hand.

"Let's show everybody our penguin dance," she said, and the two of them laughed and waddled around like penguins.

Everyone clapped and started taking pictures and videos. The people on the tram, Mr. and Mrs. Miller, the teenage boys, and the zoo officials, all had their smartphone cameras pointed at Mary Grace and Donny. The dancing went on for a long while, and the smiles went on for even longer.

Then everyone gathered to say goodbye. The family thanked the teenage boys and the zoo staff members for all their efforts in helping to find Donny. Donny gave everyone a high five and a hug.

"We have one more little surprise for you," said one of the men from the zoo, and handed Donny and Mary Grace stuffed penguins. "We want you to remember your visit and come back and see us again." To Mr. and Mrs. Miller, he handed four free zoo passes for next time. "I hope you don't mind if we post some pictures of Mary Grace and Donny's penguin dance near the penguin pool," he said.

"We'll be famous!" said Mary Grace.

Donny hugged his stuffed penguin and held it up to his ear.

"My penguin promises to remind me not to get on the train without Mary Grace when we come back," he said.

Everyone laughed and gave Donny more high fives.

"Hey, Mary Grace, nice job figuring out where your brother was!" exclaimed one of the teenage boys.

"Thanks," Mary Grace said, blushing. She was not used to getting compliments from boys.

"No, really, that was really good; it was some really smart thinking. You should be a detective." This time, it was the other teenage boy complimenting her.

"That is what we always tell her," said Mr. Miller with a proud smile. "She can solve any mystery. She is smarter than her dad, that's for sure!"

"Well, she's smarter than most high schoolers too," the first teenager concluded.

Mary Grace just kept blushing.

"Hope we see you again sometime soon," the staff said as they and the boys gave final waves and walked away.

"I think that was enough excitement for one day," Mrs. Miller said as the family passed through the exit. "I think we should go straight home, have a quick supper, and go to bed. We'll come back to the zoo soon to see the penguins."

"I'm going to walk like a normal kid to the car," Donny announced. "My legs are too tired to walk like a penguin." Donny's voice sounded tired too.

Everyone was quiet on the car ride home. Donny fell asleep in the back seat with his head on Mary Grace's lap.

At home, Mr. and Mrs. Miller started fixing dinner, and the kids plopped themselves down on the couch in front of the television. After a few minutes, Mary Grace jumped up and went over to the cabinet that held all the videos the family had collected over the years.

"I am going to look for the *Mary Poppins* video, then find the part where Bert—the chimney sweep—dances like a penguin, so we can watch it after dinner." she said.

And that is exactly what they did. Soon, the whole family was up on their feet, dancing and walking around like penguins. After lots of dancing and laughing, Mr. Miller stood up, penguin-walked right in front of the television, and announced it was time for bed. He turned off the TV while Mrs. Miller penguin-walked around the room, turning off the lights. Mary Grace and Donny waddled off to their bedrooms, throwing in a few dance steps along the way.

Soon, all the penguins were asleep.

CHAPTER

TWO

"When can we go to the zoo again?" Donny asked his mother.

"Yeah," Mary Grace chimed in, "we have free passes. Let's use them!"

"Soon, my loves," Mrs. Miller said. She was thinking about the week ahead. "Actually, we should go again before school starts."

"School starts next Monday, Mom . . . one week from tomorrow," Mary Grace said with authority.

"I know, Mary Grace. Hasn't the summer gone by quickly? We'll talk to your father about the zoo when he gets back from the last Mass today."

"Tell Dad that I promise I won't get on the train again," Donny said.

Mr. Miller had served as the priest and rector of St. James Episcopal Church for more than ten years. The Millers lived in the rectory right next to the church—which was a great place to bring up the kids. It was right across from College Hill Park and just a short drive from the Sedgwick County Zoo. Mr. Miller felt so lucky to have been assigned to a parish that could afford a full-time priest and provided full-time housing in a wonderful city like Wichita.

"Daddy, can we go to the zoo again?" Donny asked before his dad even entered the house. He and Mary Grace had been waiting for him on the porch.

"Of course, buddy . . . but we were just there yesterday," Mr. Miller said, ruffling Donny's hair and giving him a high five.

"I know . . . but we all want to go again! I promise I won't get on the train."

"Mom said we could go this week," chimed in Mary Grace, "before school starts again. "And, remember, we have free passes. Soooo . . . ?"

"Okay, okay! Let's go talk with your mom," Mr. Miller said as he opened the door.

"Mom, tell him," Mary Grace instructed her mother.

"Let me say hello first," Mrs. Miller said before turning to Mr. Miller. "Hello! How was Mass?"

"Okay. You said hello. Now tell him." Mary Grace needed an answer.

Mrs. Miller finally told him, and Mr. Miller said Friday would work best for him. He said he would get off work early and meet everyone for lunch before heading to the zoo.

"I'll help pack our lunch and make sure we have lots of cookies," said Donny, already planning for an exciting day.

"I have a better idea. I will stop and buy Snickerdoodles," Dad said, knowing they were Donny's favorites.

"Yay, Snickerdoodles!" Donny shouted, jumping in the air. "Yay, *zoo!*"

"High five, Donny. We're going to get to see the penguins again," Mary Grace said, raising her palm to meet Donny's.

That Tuesday, Mrs. Miller took Mary Grace and Donny to do some back-to-school shopping. First, they went to Target to buy school supplies, then to Towne East Square for clothes and shoes.

"Why do you need jeans with holes in them?" Mrs. Miller asked Mary Grace.

"Because all of my friends have them," replied Mary Grace.

"But why?"

"Because that's what all our favorite stars on YouTube wear."

"What stars? Would I know them?" Mrs. Miller knew she would not know any of them.

"Social influencers . . ."

"What are social influencers?"

"I don't know . . . too hard to explain, but I want jeans with holes in them."

Mrs. Miller just smiled at her honesty—and put the holey jeans in the to-buy pile they had made near the cash registers.

"Okay, now you need to pick out some clothes for those times when your favorite new holey jeans would not be appropriate."

"My new jeans would be appropriate for church though—right?" Mary Grace said, laughing. "Because they are *holey!*"

"You are a *very* witty young lady," Mrs. Miller said with pride, giving Mary Grace a playful tap on her head.

Happy with the way their trip was going, Mary Grace started picking out clothes that she knew her mother would approve of—plus one that was a little bit too grown-up.

"You actually get it. You're starting to understand that I need to pick out my own clothes," Mary Grace said.

"Thank you for seeing that even your *super-old* mother is capable of expanding her fashion horizons," Mrs. Miller said, sticking out her tongue and making a funny face. She raised her eyebrows at the grown-up top, then added, "I guess this one will go with your holey jeans."

Mrs. Miller knew that Mary Grace was growing up fast, and that pretty soon, she would not even consider being seen with her mother at the mall. She realized she would soon have to start thinking about a lot of things in a different way.

"Mo-o-om, when is it going to be *my turn?*" whined Donny.

"Right this second," said Mrs. Miller, and as soon as they finished paying for Mary Grace's purchases, off they went to find new school clothes for Donny.

He was happy with everything they selected, but that was no surprise. Donny was happy with just about everything.

"I am going to look awesome this year," he announced.

"Yes, you are, buddy. *Yes, you are.*" Mary Grace said, and she meant it.

Mary Grace was counting the days until school was to start the following week. She couldn't wait to see the friends she hadn't seen all summer—and the teachers too. She liked everything about school because she just loved figuring things out.

Donny was excited too. Although he would be in a special class, he was finally going to be at the same school as Mary Grace—Heartland Elementary—and that was a big deal.

Mrs. Miller was almost as happy as the kids that school would soon be back in session. She was a civil engineer and loved her job designing water systems for the city. During the summer, she worked from home, where she sometimes had trouble concentrating, but soon she'd be back in the office, where she belonged. Mrs. Miller loved hearing Mary Grace brag to her friends about her job. "My mom's kind of work is usually done by men," she'd say, "but Mom is really good at it."

"Let's go, Donny. Last one in the water is a rotten egg."

"Okay . . . but wait up, Mary Grace! I don't want to be a *broken* egg!"

On Friday, Mrs. Miller and the kids had packed a nice picnic lunch and left for the park just before noon. The kids were already in their swimsuits, and they headed straight for the swimming pools. Donny loved the shallow pool, which had a special ramp for people with wheelchairs. Donny would hold on to the ramp's railings with both hands and kick his feet all the way down, splashing water everywhere.

Mary Grace liked the regular pool, where she could swim quite a few laps without stopping. She had taken swimming lessons and liked to be sure she did not forget how to swim. She liked swimming, and knew she was better and faster than most kids her age. She just needed to practice a lot more. She thought that maybe someday she could join a team.

"Looking good, MG," Mr. Miller called from the side of the pool soon after he arrived.

"Thanks, Dad," she called back between strokes.

"Have you made some new friends, Donny?" Mr. Miller asked, now standing with Mrs. Miller next to the shallow pool.

"Everybody here is my friend!" shouted Donny, waving his arms all around.

"Let's go eat lunch, kids," said Mrs. Miller, and handed each one of them a towel.

They all walked across the grass to the picnic area and sat down at a low table in the shade.

"I am starving," Mr. Miller declared. "I forgot to eat anything this morning, so all I've had is coffee."

"Then, it's your own fault you're hungry, silly," Mrs. Miller said, as she handed out sandwiches to everybody.

"My favorite!" Donny said. "Peanut butter and bananas."

He took a big bite and grinned as he chewed like a pony. The peanut butter was sticking to the top of his mouth, which he always found funny.

As the family ate and talked and laughed together, Mrs. Miller felt just a little bit sad that summer vacation was ending.

"When are we going to the zoo?" Donny asked when he'd gobbled up the last bite of his sandwich, plus three cookies and a carton of juice.

"Right now," Mr. Miller said, standing up. "Everybody ready?"

"Yesss!" Donny shouted and threw his arms in the air.

"You bet!" said Mary Grace.

"Whoa," said Mrs. Miller. "We need to clean up our picnic first and throw out our trash." While she packed up the leftover food, Mr. Miller cleaned the table, Mary Grace took the trash to one of the big bins nearby, and Donny checked three times to make sure they'd remembered to pack up the leftover Snickerdoodles.

"I want to see the giraffes first," Donny said, "because they were the first thing I saw when I woke up on the train last time."

"Okay. We are going thataway." Mr. Miller pointed in the direction of the giraffes.

Soon, Donny was holding his head with both hands and trying to stretch his neck to look like a giraffe. Then, when the family went to see the monkeys, Donny watched and tried to do what they were doing. He walked around swinging his arms like the monkeys and making monkey noises.

"Donny, please don't do *everything* the monkeys do," Mary Grace said, pointing to the monkey throwing his own poop at the window. This made her parents crack up, along with other people standing nearby.

"I think we should go see the penguins now. Do you think they will remember us, Donny?" Mary Grace said as she waddled away from the monkeys, and everyone followed.

"I'm pretty sure they will," Donny replied, penguin-walking beside his sister.

"I think the ice-cream lady will remember us too," said Mr. Miller, "because we showed her how to make penguin cones."

"I'll show her again if she has forgotten," said Donny, "because I really want a penguin cone after we see the penguins." Donny was always hungry.

As it turned out, the penguins did not seem to remember them. They paid no attention, even when Donny performed his best penguin walk. Most of them just kept swimming around in the water.

"They won't look at us? Why won't they look at us?" Donny was very disappointed that the penguins didn't look at them and recognize them.

"Maybe they're just hot and tired," said Mary Grace. "Remember, it's very cold where they come from. They like snow and ice, not hot Wichita weather. Let's read more about them." Mary Grace took Donny's hand and started to lead him over to a big sign that had lots of facts about penguins.

Donny let go of Mary Grace and ran ahead. A few seconds later, he shouted back to her and his parents, "Look, look…hurry, look! They have pictures of us! They have pictures of us walking and dancing like penguins!" Donny was so excited to see the pictures that he forgot that the penguins hadn't paid any attention to him.

Sure enough, there were three pictures of Mary Grace and Donny doing their funny dance steps with the penguins in the background. Mr. and Mrs. Miller were as excited as the kids were, and both of them took pictures of the pictures. They even had Mary Grace and Donny pose next to their pictures, the way any proud parent would do.

When they were done admiring themselves, Mrs. Miller asked, "Ice cream, anyone?"

"Yesss!"

"Are you sure, Donny? You just ate two Snickerdoodles less than an hour ago." Mrs. Miller was just kidding, but Donny didn't know that.

"I'm *sure*, Mom! I want a penguin cone," he said and ran ahead toward the ice-cream lady.

"Do you remember me?" he asked her.

"Of course I remember you," the ice-cream lady said, smiling. "You were the smart little boy who taught me how to make penguin cones."

"Yes, that's me! Do you remember how to make them? Because I want one right now," Donny said.

"You mean you want one, *please*," said Mrs. Miller, "right, Donny?"

"Yes, I want one *please*," Donny repeated.

"I could never forget how to make a penguin cone," said the ice-cream lady. You taught me perfectly." She was one of those special people who made everybody feel good. She started scooping away as Donny cheered her on.

"We'll have four of those, *please*," said Mr. Miller. "Donny and Mary Grace, what do you say to the nice lady?"

"Thank yooouuu!!" they both squealed.

After she handed the cones to each of the Millers—Donny first—Mr. Miller smiled and paid her, including a little extra because she had been so kind.

CHAPTER

THREE

"And I will eat them here and there."
"Say! I will eat them ANYWHERE!"
"I do so like green eggs and ham."
"Thank you!"
"Thank you, Sam-I-am!"

Mary Grace and Donny took turns reading the last lines of one of their favorite books, their voices emphasizing every word. Then Mary Grace handed the book to Donny, who closed the cover with a *smack* as the two of them looked at each other with big smiles. This was their little tradition. It was a big deal to read an entire book, and they liked to celebrate the accomplishment.

"We really nailed it again, Donny," said Mary Grace. "We read the whole book perfectly. We are the best reading team ever. You were great." She offered up her right hand for a big high five.

Donny loved all Dr. Seuss books, but especially *Green Eggs and Ham*. Mary Grace and his parents had shared it with him so many times that he knew all the words and pictures by heart, and exactly when to turn the pages.

"We should have green eggs and ham for breakfast tomorrow," Donny said with great enthusiasm. Donny said and did everything with great enthusiasm.

"That sounds yucky," responded Mary Grace, scrunching up her nose and making a face.

"What if they're delicious? We should try them! You'll never know it's yucky if you never try it!" Donny flashed a big grin at Mary Grace.

"I don't know, Donny. . . remember what it says in the book: 'I do not like green eggs and ham! I do not like them, Sam-I-am.'"

"But Sam-I-am liked them. We might like them too!" Donny said, pleading his case.

"You like weird food," Mary Grace teased.

"I only like weird food that tastes good."

"Like peanut butter and bananas?!"

"I *love* peanut butter and bananas."

"I know you do, but it's weird."

"But *you* like it too."

"You're right; I'm weird too. I *do* like peanut butter and banana sandwiches. Okay, we'll make green eggs and ham.

We'll ask Mom if she will help us make green eggs and ham in the morning. And even *I* will try them."

"Yesss!" Donny said, raising his arms in victory.

"I have to go now, Donny," Mary Grace said as she jumped off Donny's bed.

"Where are you going?" Donny asked, disappointed.

"I told Stacy I would go over to her house. We might swim in her pool, so I'm going to bring my bathing suit."

"Awww, you are a lucky ducky! You're going to have the best day ever."

"I'm sorry you can't come along, buddy, but I will be back before dinner, and maybe we can play marbles. Meanwhile, you should ask Dad if he wants to play baseball outside. I bet he'd love that. Grab your bat and glove, and go ask him."

"Okay, but . . . can you help me find my bat? And . . . my glove?"

Mary Grace was a good sister, so even though she was in a hurry, she said, "Sure, buddy—but then I have to go."

It was a Saturday afternoon in October, but the temperature had been in the eighties for the past few days. It was what some people, like Mr. and Mrs. Miller, liked to call an *Indian summer.* School was in full swing, and Mary Grace was enjoying life to the fullest.

She could not imagine having a more perfect life than she had right at that moment.

Mary Grace's hair was still wet when she came home. As she passed Donny sitting on the couch, she waved.

"When you get dry, can we play the marble game?" Donny loved to play games with his marbles.

Mary Grace knew that Donny loved to set up dominoes on the floor, and then have a contest with Mary Grace to see who could knock down the most dominoes with a marble. Donny usually won.

"Sure." Mary Grace said. "I'll be back in ten minutes."

When she got to the kitchen door, she called out to her parents, "Hi! I'm home, and I'm going to take a shower!"

"Okay, dear. I hope you had fun," her mom said in a voice that sounded different somehow.

Something did not seem right to Mary Grace. Her mom appeared distracted. Her parents were hunched over the kitchen table, having some kind of serious talk. She couldn't make out what they were saying, but her mom's voice kept cracking.

As she showered, Mary Grace got a funny feeling in her stomach, and her heart felt like it was beating faster than normal. Her mind started racing.

Was mom crying?

Why?

Was somebody sick?

Did somebody they know get hurt?

Who?

Or . . . was it something worse?

She was scared it was bad news. *Divorce?* Her good friend Caroline's parents had just told Caroline they were going to get a divorce, and everybody in that family had been sad and angry for weeks.

She got out of the shower, dried off, and changed into shorts and a fresh T-shirt. As she brushed the knots out of her hair, Mary Grace was still worrying about why her mom might be crying. She took a deep breath and headed to the kitchen to find out what was going on.

Mary Grace took one final deep breath as she approached the kitchen.

"This is going to be so hard on the children."

She peeked into the kitchen and saw that her mom was on the phone while her dad was sitting at the kitchen table with his laptop open, staring out the window. Mrs. Miller looked up, and when she saw Mary Grace, she quicky got off the phone and went to the sink.

She doesn't want me to see how upset she is, thought Mary Grace, who was always good at figuring things out.

"Mary Grace," her mom called out, "would you please go get Donny? Your father and I would like to talk with both of you."

Uh-oh.

Mary Grace did as she was told, hoping that whatever her parents wanted to talk about, it wouldn't upset her brother. But what was it? Everything had seemed fine just a few hours earlier. The summer had been great . . . but then again, Caroline had thought everything was fine with *her* parents, and look how that turned out.

"Are we going to play marble games now?" Donny asked eagerly as Mary Grace entered his room.

"Not right now, buddy. First, we have to go talk with Mom and Dad." She gave Donny a big hug, told him to leave his iPad in his room, and led him to the kitchen.

Mom and Dad were sitting at the kitchen table and stared at them as they walked in. Mr. Miller closed his laptop, stood up, and hugged Mrs. Miller. He then hugged Mary Grace and picked up Donny and hugged him long and hard before everybody sat down at the table.

"Guys, . . . your mother and I need to talk to you about . . . Africa."

"Africa!?" Mary Grace asked, standing up. For some reason, Mary Grace was more scared than she was before.

"Who is Africa?" Donny asked innocently.

Mr. Miller looked at Mrs. Miller, who was blowing her nose into a tissue.

That nose-blow gave Mary Grace goose bumps. She knew bad news was coming. She just wanted time to stand still or, better yet, go backward.

"Your mom and I have been given an unusual assignment," Mr. Miller said slowly, looking first at Mary Grace and then at Donny. "The bishop spoke with me a few days ago. He would like us to be missionaries for the Episcopal Church in Africa. We would go to a small village in Kenya that needs a priest and teacher like me. Your mom would help the villagers get clean drinking water. We'd be gone for two years."

Mary Grace and Donny just blinked. They didn't know what to say, or even ask.

"Your father and I have talked about it a lot and have decided to go, even though we know it will be hard for the two of you."

"This was the hardest decision your mother and I have ever had to make," Mr. Miller added.

For a minute, nobody said anything.

Finally, Mary Grace spoke: "Are you saying that we are *all* going to live in Africa for *two years?*"

"Where is Africa?" Donny asked innocently.

"Africa is far away, Donny," Mrs. Miller said, then turned to Mary Grace. "And no, my love. We wouldn't all be going to Africa. It's important that both of you stay in school and keep doing all the things that children do. Just your father and I are going to Africa, while you two—"

"But who's going to take care of us?" asked Mary Grace, sounding panicked.

"We talked to Grandma Cathy and Papa Steve in California, and they would love to have you come and stay with them at their ranch."

"For two years?!"

"Your father is right: this is the hardest decision we've ever had to make in our lives," Mrs. Miller tried to explain.

"But for two years?!"

"It could be less . . ." Mrs. Miller offered as she looked down guiltily at the table.

"Seriously, Mom . . . you can't really mean you are going to leave us and go all the way to Kenya for two years?! And send Donny and me to California? *FOR TWO YEARS?*" Mary Grace stared at her parents, her face as white as a sheet. She was fighting back tears, and when Donny saw this, his own lip trembled as if he were about to cry. "Mom!" she continued, "I thought you were going to tell us you were getting a divorce, but this is even *worse*. This is *much worse*. It's like you're getting a divorce from Donny and me!"

Unable to hold back her tears any longer, Mary Grace ran to her room and slammed the door.

"What is 'getting a divorce'?" Donny asked innocently.

CHAPTER

FOUR

With two very upset and confused children on their hands, Mr. and Mrs. Miller decided they should divide and conquer. Mr. Miller stayed with Donny, while Mrs. Miller headed toward Mary Grace's bedroom.

"You and your sister are going to California, bud. Isn't that great?" Mr. Miller asked Donny.

"I . . . guess . . . but then why is Mary Grace crying?" Donny asked, concerned about his sister.

"Oh, you know how hard Mary Grace thinks about everything. And sometimes it takes her a little while to get used to new things. All I know is, you two are going to have great fun on the ranch with Grandma Cathy and Papa Steve!"

"And Krug and Toby," Donny added. He loved his grandparents' dogs.

"That's right! You'll get to play with the dogs every day."

"And maybe we can ride horses again, like last time," Donny said, a smile creeping across his face.

"Of course you can. And there are so many fun things to do in California that you haven't even tried yet."

"Yeah, California is fun," Donny declared.

"That's right. The ranch is fun. The beach is fun. A new school with new teachers and new friends can be fun. California is fun," Mr. Miller said, emphasizing the word *fun* four times.

"I can't wait to go back!" Donny seemed like he was ready to get on the plane.

Mrs. Miller knocked gently on Mary Grace's bedroom door.

"Don't come in."

"It's Mom, honey. We need to talk a little more."

"No, we don't. There is nothing to talk about."

"Yes, there is . . ."

"No! You and Dad just *decide* things. It's not fair! What if I don't *want* you to go to Africa? Will you change your mind?"

"Sweetheart, I know this seems very sudden, but I want to explain why we are going and why it is so important. I think once you hear the whole story, you will understand much better. But most of all, I want you to know that you will be fine without us for a little while. You will be fine and safe and happy—and very loved—in California."

"If you think Donny and I are going to be *fine* and *happy* leaving Wichita and moving to California, you're totally wrong! This whole thing sucks, and it's *so unfair!*"

"Come on, dear . . . please open up, and let's talk. Your grandparents are so excited to have the time with you and Donny. I know this is difficult—believe me, it is for your father and I too, but—"

Mrs. Miller was interrupted by Mary Grace. "Please go away. This just *sucks*. Leave me alone," Mary Grace said, her voice cracking.

"Mary Grace, I will leave you some time to think, but please also think about your grandparents. They love you and Donny so much. If they heard you speaking like this, it would really hurt their feelings. They can't wait to make fun memories with you and Donny."

Mrs. Miller heard Mary Grace's sobs and backed away from the door.

There was a long silence followed by a second knock on Mary Grace's door.

"No! I said you can't come in."

"It's me, your brother," replied Donny.

"Oh, okay, Donny, you can come in. Just not Mom."

Donny opened the door a crack and looked in. When he saw his sister spread out across her bed, crying, he pushed it open wider and ran to her, enfolding her in a big hug. Mary Grace hugged him back very hard.

"Why are you so sad?" Donny asked.

"Because Mom and Dad have decided you and I are moving to California to live with Grandma Cathy and Papa Steve."

Donny thought for a few seconds, then smiled.

"But . . . that will be so cool, Mary Grace. We love it there! We can see Toby and Krug all the time, and ride horses, and—"

"You just don't get it," Mary Grace interjected. "It's going to be the worst thing that has ever happened to us."

"It . . . is? Why?" asked Donny.

Mary Grace knew Donny would never fully understand, and she realized there was no point in making him as sad and angry as she was.

"I wish I was more like you, Donny," she said, and she meant every word of it.

After lying on her bed, cuddling with Donny for a long while, Mary Grace got up and asked Donny to stay in her room. She told him that he could play with her stuffed animals.

"Really? Can I? You usually don't want me to touch them."

"That's because you usually have dirt or peanut butter on your hands."

"Look," he said, raising his palms to her, fingers spread wide, "clean hands."

"Very clean." Mary Grace said, as she inspected his hands, "Okay . . . play with anything you want."

"Really? Anything?"

"Yes. Anything."

"Even your favorites? The ones I *never* get to touch?"

"Even my favorites, Donny," Mary Grace assured him.

"Yesss!" said Donny, raising his arms triumphantly.

Certain things did not seem so important to Mary Grace anymore.

Mary Grace walked toward the kitchen, not really knowing what she wanted to say, but that did not stop her from opening her mouth as soon as she saw her parents at the table.

"I think this is a rotten thing for you to do to Donny and me," she began. "This is my last year at Heartland Elementary, and I won't be able to graduate with my friends. This is for *two whole years.* My life is being ruined, and you don't even seem to care." After taking a breath, she continued, "I guess this means you totally hate me. It's just like when you wouldn't let me get my ears pierced for my birthday!"

That last thing sounded kind of lame, she thought. *But, oh well . . . I said it!*

The look on her parents' faces showed how much her words hurt.

"You know we don't hate you. You must know how much we love you and Donny. But this is something we think we simply need to do," her father said, using his calm priest voice.

Ignoring the compliment, Mary Grace went on: "But, Dad! Why is it so important? And, why are Donny and I so *un*important?"

"Honey, you and Donnie are the most important people in our lives. And if we didn't truly believe that you would be safe and happy with your grandparents, we could never consider fulfilling this mission."

Mary Grace crossed her arms and looked at the floor. It was her mom's turn to take a shot at reasoning with her.

"Sweetheart, this is not easy for us. It was a really hard and scary decision to make, but we believe it's the right one. It is not often that people get a chance to make a real difference in this world. This is our chance."

Mary Grace couldn't help it; she began listening and trying to make sense of what her parents were telling her.

"Your father will be doing God's work for these people. He will be teaching them useful skills and giving them faith and hope. And I will be giving them clean water. Water is a basic human need. In America, we take it for granted. Water is all they have to drink. They can't just go to the fridge and grab a Coke when they're thirsty. They don't have refrigerators.

They don't have Coke. And right now, they don't have clean water. These people could die. Your father and I may be able to help save them. This is important work—*very* important work. This is not about Coke and pierced ears; it is about life and death."

"Okay, okay, I get it! But why does it have to be you two? Can't *somebody else* go save lives in Kenya? Somebody who doesn't have kids who want to stay in Wichita, where they belong?"

"Because, Mary Grace, your father and I have been chosen by the church and the World Health Organization for this task. We have the skills they need. Not somebody else—*us.*"

Mary Grace had been listening closely. She understood that her parents thought they had good reasons to go to Africa. But she only saw it from her perspective. She only saw how their decision affected *her.* She did not want to come across as some little spoiled brat, but she had to find someone to blame for her misery.

"I hate the church!" she shouted. "The church is ruining my life. If we do go to California, I'm not packing any church clothes because I'm never going to church again as long as I live!" She continued, "The church told you guys to go to Africa? The church obviously doesn't care about me, so why should I care about the church? I'm never going to church again as long as I live!"

Mr. and Mrs. Miller looked at each other but said nothing. They both understood that sometimes kids need to get all their feelings out—and this was one of those times.

"Anyway, I read online that the only people who go to church in California are celebrities looking for photo ops," Mary Grace continued her rant, "and weird people who go to churches where the people practice witchcraft and handle snakes and believe that they can cure all diseases." She was on a roll. "The weirdos out there will probably try to cure Donny's Down syndrome with spells and snakebites. Is that what you want? For Donny to get *attacked by snakes?*"

"Honey, I think you are getting a little carried away," said Mr. Miller quietly. He reminded her, "We went to an Episcopal church when we visited your grandparents in California before, and you liked it—remember? Do you remember Father Randall and his husband, Bill, from the church last summer?"

Mary Grace thought for a moment, and then said, "Yeah, okay, I will admit that church was pretty cool. They had movie nights and parties that were fun. And they had special breakfasts for kids, and classes that were outdoors in the park. They even had a special bowl full of water for dogs during Mass, because some dogs came to church with their families."

"See . . . not all churches in California are weird." Mr. Miller had made his point, but he continued, "Grandma Cathy and Papa Steve told me that Father Randall, Bill, and their dog come to dinner at their ranch a lot. I just hope Father Randall and Bill don't like tuna casserole or red Jell-O, like Episcopalians in Wichita."

"I think tuna casserole is a Wichita thing, Dad. At least, I hope so . . . *blech!*"

"Yeah, *blech!*" Donny exclaimed, copying Mary Grace.

Mr. Miller laughed and stuck out his tongue as if he were sick.

"I don't like tuna casserole or red Jell-O either, but when you are the priest, you have to eat a lot of things you don't like."

This got a smile and a little laugh out of Mary Grace, even though she did not want to laugh. *This was not a laughing matter.*

"Mary Grace, do you remember the name of Father Randall and Bill's dog?"

"Ike," she replied, "and I know why they named him that. It's for President Dwight D. Eisenhower, who was a famous general in the Second World War before becoming president. *Ike* was his nickname—"

"*AND,*" Donny interrupted Mary Grace, "he grew up in Abilene, Kansas! Did you know that?"

"That's right! You both have a very good memory," said Mrs. Miller, who had been quiet up to that point.

Mary Grace thought for a moment, then said, "I want to know something. If Kansas was good enough for

Eisenhower—who was a big-deal general and then a famous president—why isn't it good enough for us to just stay here?"

"Oh, sweetie, I think you know the answer to that," said Mrs. Miller. "You know we aren't leaving Kansas because we don't like it or because it isn't good enough. We are leaving because we know we can make a difference somewhere else."

"And because you don't like tuna casserole?!" Mary Grace said, finally summoning up a genuine laugh.

Relieved by her change in mood, Mr. and Mrs. Miller laughed too—and suddenly, all of the anger left the room. Smiles were exchanged all around . . . but nothing could take away the sadness they all felt at the thought of leaving home and one another.

Tears streamed down Mary Grace's face.

"I am going to miss you guys so much."

CHAPTER
FIVE

The Millers hugged one another and cried for quite a while before anyone said more, but it was Mrs. Miller who finally broke the silence.

"Thank you for hearing us out, Mary Grace. That is what a mature young woman would do—what a grown-up would do. You continue to amaze Dad and me every day."

Mary Grace looked at the floor. She never knew what to say when somebody paid her a compliment.

"We know you will probably still feel angry about this sometimes—with us and with the church—but don't ever think for one second that we don't love you. Don't lose faith in us."

"And don't lose faith in the church, either, honey," Mr. Miller added.

"I might not be able to help it, Dad," Mary Grace replied. "The church is on my official poop list now for sending you guys away." Tears were welling up in her eyes again.

"Ah, Mary Grace," her dad said, with a sigh, "I guess you are learning that life takes strange twists and turns. God works in mysterious ways. And, you know what? This may turn out to be a really good thing for all of us." He was sounding a lot like a priest, probably because he *was* a priest.

"I doubt it, Dad. I mean . . . it will probably be a good thing for those village people . . . but not for *us*," Mary Grace said. She was not buying her dad's evaluation of the situation.

"One thing you should know," said Mrs. Miller, "is that we will be coming to California for as many visits as they allow. You'll be able to show us all the things you've discovered in California and tell us about all your new friends and experiences when we come to visit. We promise we'll only be in Africa for two years . . . or maybe even less. And, of course, we'll write lots of letters and emails and have FaceTime phone calls whenever we can."

Mary Grace said, "I just wish both of you would stay in Wichita. I wish we could *all* just stay in Wichita."

"I want you to know that going to Africa will be hard for all of us," Mr. Miller added sincerely, "especially for your mother, who I am absolutely sure would rather stay in Wichita."

"Why? Because she's the only one in the family who likes tuna casserole?!" Mary Grace joked, providing comic relief once again.

They all had another good laugh, despite the seriousness of the conversation.

"I want to talk a little bit about Donny now," Mrs. Miller said, her tone turning serious. "He is a happy, positive kid, and we never want that to change. So I am counting on you, Mary Grace; for Donny's sake, starting now, we all need to try to say only positive things about California."

"It would be a lot easier to say positive things about California if we could live someplace cool, like Malibu or San Francisco—or maybe Beverly Hills. Like all the celebrities." Mary Grace raised her nose in the air, pretending to be snooty.

"Very funny. But seriously, if you want to complain and vent your emotions to me or your dad, that's okay. But let's all try not to be negative in front of Donny. Let's all be positive about everything for Donny."

"You're right, Mom. Of course I want Donny to be happy, like he always is. I'll try . . . but being positive all the time isn't going to be easy . . . because this all just *sucks*."

Mary Grace slowly opened her bedroom door. She saw Donny playfully hugging and talking to her stuffed animals.

When he saw his sister, he smiled.

"I took good care of your animals," he announced.

"Thank you. They all look very happy."

"They *are* happy."

"What were you talking with them about? They didn't tell you any of my secrets, did they?" Mary Grace liked kidding with Donny.

"Yes! Yes, they did! . . . They told me secrets! They told me funny things about you."

"They *did?* Oh no! What did they say about me?"

"Well . . ." he said, thinking for a minute, "they said you snore when you sleep." Donny laughed and made a snoring sound.

Mary Grace picked up a stuffed panda bear—her favorite—and spoke directly to it: "Do I snore in my sleep?"

She made her panda bear nod its head.

"Pancham Panda says I snore, Donny, so I guess I do. Panda always tells the truth."

Donny laughed and laughed.

"Guess what else they told me?" Donny asked, warming to the game.

"What?"

"They said you pick your nose when you sleep!" He laughed uncontrollably.

"What?! Ewwww, gross! Did they really say that?" Mary Grace exclaimed, acting surprised.

With one quick dive, Mary Grace tackled Donny and began piling all of the animals on top of him while he wriggled and laughed and pushed them off. After a few minutes of this silliness, they both fell back, exhausted and giggling. Finally, Donny looked into his sister's eyes, from about three inches away.

"Are you still sad?"

The truth was, Mary Grace *was* still sad—and still a little angry too. After Donny left her room to get ready for bed, she started calling all her friends to share the terrible news. She was moving far away and her parents were going even farther. The church had decided to ruin her life, and there was nothing she could do about it.

Much to Mary Grace's dismay, her parents did not change their minds about being missionaries in Africa for two years—and the next few weeks were crazy. Mom spent a lot of time packing and mailing packages of clothes, toys, and books to California. She also packed up things for Africa, but the majority of the family's life went into storage.

Donny was not much help with the packing, but he did want to do something special for Mary Grace.

"Mom," he said, "I need your help. Please tell me all the things Mary Grace and I liked last summer in California. I want to draw pictures of them all and make a book for her so she'll get excited and happy about our trip."

Overhearing this, Mr. Miller suggested to Mary Grace that she write down all the things she liked about Wichita, especially the things she knew she would miss the most.

"That would be a loooooong list, Dad," she replied, and went back to her packing.

Donny and Mrs. Miller started working on his list at the kitchen table. Each time Donny remembered something—like his grandparents' dogs, the horses they'd ridden, the beach with the elephant seals, and the pond where the ducks lived—Mrs. Miller would write it at the bottom of a piece of paper.

"This is a great list, Donny," she told him. "Mary Grace is going to love your picture book."

Mrs. Miller then remembered something Grandma Cathy had told her. "You know what I just thought of, Donny?" she asked. "Your grandma told me that a few years ago, a penguin named Lucky was born at the Santa Barbara Zoo in California, where Grandma and Grandpa live. His right foot didn't work the way it was supposed to, so a company that made sandals volunteered to make a special boot for Lucky. When they put the boot on Lucky, he could walk and climb like all the other penguins. I think I am going to write 'Lucky' on a piece of paper so you can draw a picture of something you haven't seen yet."

"That's cool, Mom," said Donny. "There was a girl in my class last year—Angela—who had to wear a special shoe, just like Lucky, to help her walk. Maybe if we go see Lucky in California, Mary Grace can take a picture of him, and I can send it to Angela."

Donny decided to start with the picture of Lucky.

When he finished it to his satisfaction, he put it aside, pointed at the list, and asked, "What does this one say, Mom?" He asked this each time he grabbed a new piece of paper.

"Your book will certainly make Mary Grace happier about moving. We will make it really special for her. Be sure to tell her about Lucky and his special shoe, so she has something to look forward to seeing in California," Mrs. Miller suggested.

"Do you think I should give her some of my most special marbles as well?" Donny asked. He was very generous when it came to his big sister.

"That is a nice idea, Donny, but I think you should hold on to those yourself. You can put your favorite ones right into your suitcase so you know where they are the minute you get to Grandma and Grandpa's."

Donny didn't tell his mother, but he had already packed *all* his marbles in his suitcase—which made it pretty heavy and hard to lift. He hoped no one would notice.

Mary Grace took a break from packing. She was almost done, and had decided to make the list her dad had suggested, after all. She was constantly thinking of all the things she would miss about Wichita, so she figured she might as well write them down.

She wrote "Missing Wichita" at the top of a page in her notebook with the pug on the front, and then started writing and writing and writing some more. She had been right when she'd told her dad the list would be long. There were so many great things about where she lived. She would *definitely* miss living in Wichita.

SIX

B y the time Mary Grace finished, her "Missing Wichita" list was four pages long. She'd listed anything and everything she could think of, and thoughts continued to flow through her head. Her list included the many lakes in and around her town, where she loved to swim and play on the beach. *I love water,* she thought. *And beaches. I know California has water too, but it's saltwater. With sharks. And jellyfish.* She shivered at the thought of yucky jellyfish.

She had also included the Wichita Riverfest. *Does California have festivals too?* she wondered. The Wichita Riverfest was a big event that was held twice a year—once at the beginning of summer and once at the end, and it always seemed to be one of the highlights of each year. She'd always loved the Welcome Summer Parade at the end of the

Riverfest, especially seeing Windwagon Smith, a man who dressed up like an old-time admiral and rode a schooner on wheels. *Does California have parades?* she wondered. She had heard of something called the Rose Parade, where all the floats were made of flowers, but it couldn't be better than the Welcome Summer Parade.

The other thing Mary Grace loved about the Riverfest came at the end of the parade. Jets from McConnell Air Force Base would fly over everyone's heads with red, white, and blue smoke coming out of them in long streams. She didn't know how they did that, but she was sure there was nothing like it in California.

Of course, she had included in her list the Sedgwick County Zoo. Walking like penguins with Donny, riding the zoo tram, and eating penguin ice-cream cones were all there in her notebook. *I really hope the Santa Barbara Zoo is even half as good,* she thought.

Reading over the list she'd made was like reliving her whole life in Wichita. It made her very glad she'd taken her dad's suggestion.

"What are you doing, honey?" Mrs. Miller asked Mary Grace from the doorway of her room.

"Nothing. Just writing down all the stuff that I'll miss about Wichita. Dad told me I should."

"Can I see it?"

"Not yet, Mom. It's not even close to being done—only four pages so far . . . single spaced." Mary Grace wanted to make her point that she was going to miss Wichita.

"I know there are a lot of things you will miss. I would love to read it when you are done." She paused, then added, "I'm going to miss Wichita too." After another pause, she said, "You know, your brother has been working very hard on a surprise for you. And when you see it, I want you to ask him about Lucky the Penguin at the Santa Barbara Zoo. He has a special problem and a special solution that Donny is eager to tell you about."

"Sure, Mom. I already know I want to take Donny to the zoo there. We can go see Lucky."

"Get ready for dinner, honey; we'll be eating in a few minutes."

When her mom left, Mary Grace tucked the notebook into her backpack that was going on the plane with her. She still wasn't happy about leaving Wichita, but she was starting to get used to the idea. She had to admit that she was looking forward to seeing her grandparents and their dogs—and maybe even Lucky the Penguin.

"I will miss swimming in the pool at Stacy's house and at the park."

Mary Grace was in her room with her mother, packing a few last items, including her bathing suits and flip-flops. The flight to California was the next day.

"Remember Grandma's friend Gigi?" Mrs. Miller asked her daughter.

"Sure, Mom. She's the one who lives in that nice place for older people, with the big pool."

"Right! Well, Grandma and Gigi and their friends play bridge there every Thursday, and I bet you and Donny will be able to go along and swim in that pool."

"But they're all really old, Mom. They probably don't even own bathing suits—and I'm sure they have no idea how to play Marco Polo." Mary Grace scoffed.

"Maybe you and Donny can teach them. I think they might enjoy playing some swimming games with you guys."

"Is Gigi's condo the place where Mrs. Knight lives with her son?"

"Yes, that's right. Mrs. Knight runs the building, and Ed helps her."

Mary Grace remembered that she and Donny had met Ed when they were in California last summer, and Donny was impressed that Ed had a marble collection that was probably in the thousands.

"At least Donny will have a friend who loves marbles as much as he does. I just hope I can find some friends too," Mary Grace said with some doubt in her voice.

"I'm sure you will, honey. Once you get to know your classmates, you can invite them to the ranch. Grandma and Papa would be happy to have some young people around to play with the dogs and maybe ride horses."

"Are these friends who Grandma Cathy plays bridge with the same friends she calls the Grandma Gang?" Mary Grace asked her mother.

"I think so. Honestly, Grandma has so many friends that it's hard to keep track of them!"

Mary Grace had seen the picture of Grandma Cathy and her friends in a newspaper clipping her mother had shown her.

"All I know is that the Grandma Gang once helped the police solve a mystery at the 7-Eleven store near the ranch," she said. "But you guys never told me exactly what happened. I've never heard of a bunch of old people forming a gang and getting their picture in the paper!"

Mrs. Miller sighed.

"If you want to know the whole story, I'll pull out that clipping again," she said, and went to fetch it from a box in her bedroom closet.

When she came back, she and Mary Grace climbed up on her bed and snuggled close. Mrs. Miller leaned back against the headboard and prepared to tell the story of the Grandma Gang. Suddenly, something occurred to her.

"You know what?" she asked Mary Grace.

"What, Mom?? Go on!"

"I think you should hear this story directly from Grandma Cathy." Mrs. Miller said, sure that would be the right thing to do. "She loves to tell this story and would really love telling it to her granddaughter. When you get out there, ask her. It will give the two of you something to talk about as you get to know each other again. I hadn't thought about it before, but you two have so much in common! You are both very smart and love solving mysteries."

"Awww, I want to hear it *now*."

"It will give you something to look forward to."

"Okay, Mom. I can wait. You're right. I'll like hearing it directly from Grandma. She will have all the details, and I like details."

"Oh, I know you do. But be careful when you meet Grandma's friends, and don't let that inquisitive mind run wild. For heaven's sake, *don't* ask to hear details about their grandchildren."

"Why not, Mom?"

"Because they all just *love* bragging about them. Those ladies have so many pictures of their grandchildren on their cell phones, you could go cross-eyed looking at them all. So . . ." Mrs. Miller stopped, and looked Mary Grace straight in the eye. "Don't ever ask any of the Grandma Gang about their grandchildren unless you have hours to look at all the pictures and hear every detail about their lives." Mrs. Miller laughed, and so did Mary Grace.

"Okay, got it. NO grandchildren. Even I don't like details *that* much."

Mrs. Miller and Mary Grace laughed and laughed, and then hugged and hugged.

"Boy, am I going to miss *you*, sweetheart," Mrs. Miller said, and the tears started flowing all over again.

CHAPTER

SEVEN

As he drove to Dwight D. Eisenhower National Airport, Mr. Miller kept looking at Mary Grace and Donny in the rearview mirror. He knew this was the last time he would see his children for a very long time, and he was already missing them.

Mary Grace was busy texting on her new iPhone. She had been begging for one for years, and her parents had told her that they might give her one for graduation from elementary school. But things changed, and they realized that she would need a good phone to keep in touch with her friends back in Kansas, communicate with her grandparents, and, of course, keep in touch with them. Mr. Miller had given her his phone, and the church had gotten him one designed especially for international calling.

Mary Grace didn't care that her new phone was almost two years old. It was now her most prized possession, and the happiness it gave her made her parents happy too.

Mary Grace put down her phone and looked out the window at Wichita for one last time. She knew that life for she and Donny was about to change in a big way—and she also knew that life for her parents was going to change in an even bigger way. Her mom and dad were going to Africa. She and Donny were going to California. Big difference. She was worried for her parents, just like they were worried for her.

At the airport, Donny and Mary Grace watched the baggage handler straining to pull Donny's suitcase onto the conveyor belt.

"I packed my whole marble collection," Donny whispered in his sister's ear. And then, louder, he said, "Bye, marbles! See you in California!"

When it was time for the two of them to board the plane, Mary Grace and her mother hugged forever. They tried not to cry, but tears came anyway. Only Donny was happy.

He gave each of his parents a big hug and declared, "This is one of the best days of my life!"

This put smiles on the faces of his family members and everybody else who heard it. Donny had that effect on people.

As the kids disappeared down the jet bridge, Mrs. Miller said, "I know we told Mary Grace to take good care of Donny, but I think it might end up being the other way around."

"We're lucky to have such good kids," Mrs. Miller said as they turned to leave.

"You definitely have that right," Mr. Miller said with tears now streaming down his face.

"I call window!" shouted Donny as the flight attendant showed them to their seats near the front of the plane. As soon as he was buckled in, he began staring out the window. "Hey, Mary Grace, look!" he said. "They're putting bags on the plane."

"That's right, buddy. See if you can spot ours."

"They all look the same."

"I guess ... but remember that yours is the heaviest with all those marbles! So look for one that is hard to lift!"

They both laughed.

Donny kept a lookout as the plane wheeled down the runway, picking up speed and finally climbing into the sky. After a few more minutes, they broke through the clouds, and the bright sun streamed in. Donny loved looking down at the fluffy clouds—which reminded him of cotton candy— and seeing mountains and cities through the breaks in them.

Once the pilot announced that they could take their seatbelts off, Mary Grace rummaged through her backpack and pulled out her list, "Missing Wichita"—but then she decided that reading it would make her too sad, and put it back. She wanted to stay excited and positive for Donny's sake. Her mom had told her this was important, and that it would help make her happy too. She hoped her mom was right.

The flight attendants took very good care of Mary Grace and Donny for the whole five hours of the flight. One of them gave Donny a special pin with airplane wings on it and helped him pin it to his shirt. Another one brought them Cokes and little bags of pretzels.

"This is one of the best days of my life," Donny told everyone sitting around them. "We are going to see our grandparents and their dogs, Toby and Krug. They live in California."

He showed the people sitting near them the animal treats he had brought with him for Toby and Krug, and told them about the marbles in his suitcase. Everyone was very nice to Donny—except one old man who was trying to sleep. After he'd shushed Donny a couple of times, Donny quieted down and started looking out the window again.

"Hey, Donny," said Mary Grace, "look what I brought." She pulled their copy of *Green Eggs and Ham* out of her backpack.

"Hey, that's one of my favorites," said a man sitting across the aisle.

"My favorite book ever," said Donny.

As Mary Grace started reading the Dr. Seuss book aloud, people started reciting along with her. Everybody seemed to know it by heart, although a few people were reading it from their phones. Everybody was smiling as they recited the rhymes together. By the end, it seemed as if half the people on the plane had joined in.

> And I will eat them here and there.
> Say! I will eat them ANYWHERE!
> I do so like green eggs and ham.
> Thank you!
> Thank you, Sam-I-am!

Everyone recited the last lines slowly, word by word, and at peak volume. Then something special happened: the entire plane erupted into applause.

When the applause died down, Donny unbuckled his seatbelt, kneeled on his seat, and looked around at all the faces on the airplane. People waved to him, and he waved back.

"This really *is* the best day of my life," he proclaimed.

The flight attendant came by one last time to make sure everyone was buckled up.

"Remember to keep sitting in your seat even after we land," she told Mary Grace and Donny. "Wait here for me, and I'll help you find your grandparents. They are going to be waiting for you right by the airport door."

When the plane came to a stop, everybody but Donny jumped up and started pulling bags and bundles down from the storage bins over their heads. As they filed past the two children, many of them had kind words to say.

"Thank you for reminding me how much I love Dr. Seuss," said one lady.

Another one said, "You two are very well-behaved children. I hope you enjoy your vacation."

It seemed like everyone on the plane said something to Mary Grace and Donny on their way past them, and Donny held his hand up high and received lots of high fives.

Mary Grace was in good spirits as the two of them followed the flight attendant off the plane and through the little tunnel to the airport. Sure enough, Grandma Cathy and Papa Steve were waiting there.

"Grandma!" shouted Donny, nearly knocking her down with a big hug.

"Hello, my two loves," said Grandma.

"Hey there, sport," said Papa Steve.

The four of them walked down a long hallway and took an escalator down to the place where their bags were going around and around on a special machine called a *carousel*—just like the merry-go-round in the park. A man in a uniform helped them get their bags down and put them on two carts. Donny noticed that he had to use two hands for his suitcase—and elbowed Mary Grace in the ribs.

"My marbles made it to California," he said.

"Before we head to the car, I think you two might want to change into something more comfortable," Grandma Cathy suggested.

"Mom made us wear these clothes," said Mary Grace, "so we'd look nice when we saw you. I wanted to wear just plain old jeans. She insisted that we dress for the plane like we were dressing for church." It was obvious Mary Grace was not pleased with what she was wearing.

"Well, never you mind! You do look very nice—but I brought some clothes that are a bit better suited to our weather here." She handed each of them a shopping bag.

"Wow. Thanks," Mary Grace said before looking in the bag.

"There's a family restroom right over there, where you can both get changed. I'll wait outside, and Papa Steve will stay here with the bags."

As they walked toward the restroom, Donny reached into his gift bag and pulled out khaki shorts and a T-shirt that read, "I love California."

"The best day of my life is even better now," Donny said as he followed after his sister.

Mary Grace's T-shirt and shorts were similar to Donny's, but his shirt was green, and hers was purple—her favorite color.

"Ta-da! Don't I look great?" Donny said as he emerged from a stall. "You look great too, Mary Grace!"

When they all rejoined Papa Steve, he said, "Wow! You are real California kids now!"

Grandma Cathy sensed that Mary Grace wasn't as happy as her brother.

"Does everything fit okay, sweetie?" she asked.

"It's all great, Grandma. Really," Mary Grace replied quietly, with little enthusiasm.

"What's the matter, dear?" Grandma Cathy knew something was bothering her granddaughter.

"It's just that . . . it reminds me that we are not in Kansas anymore."

Grandma Cathy gave her a big hug and whispered in her ear, "You can always turn it inside out."

CHAPTER

EIGHT

P apa Steve groaned as he tried to lift Donny's suitcase into the trunk of the car.

"What's in this bag?" he asked. "Did you kids bring rocks from Kansas?"

"I brought all my marbles," Donny said proudly, with a big grin across his face.

"I'll help you," said Mary Grace, grabbing on to one end of the bag. She thought she heard Papa Steve muttering under his breath something about *hundreds of pounds of marbles.*

"Did you remember to pack some clothes too?" Papa Steve asked Donny, who laughed at his silly question.

"Mom packed my clothes first," he said. "Then I put the marbles on top of them."

"You know, Donny," said Grandma Cathy, "our friend Ed loves to play marbles. He's a little older than you—going to be seventeen this year—but he still loves his marbles."

"I know!" said Donny. "I remember him. He's Gigi's son. I will take some of my marbles when we go visit them."

Mary Grace saw something big and furry scratching against the car window. "Look, Donny, it's Krug!" she shouted.

"Yesss!" Donny yelped, smacking his hand against the glass in a high five with Krug.

"We thought you two would enjoy it if Krug was part of your welcoming party," said Grandma Cathy, as she opened the door to let out the fluffy, black cockapoo.

"Look, Krugie, I brought treats for you and Toby," said Donny pulling a couple of dog biscuits out of his pocket.

Grandma and Papa waited patiently while Mary Grace and Donny petted and hugged Krug and tossed treats in the air for him to catch.

"Where is Toby?" Donny asked, when he had no more treats left to toss.

"Oh, Donny…" said Papa Steve quietly, "I'm afraid I have some sad news about Toby. He was a very old dog, you know, and he got sick. He died a few months ago, but, we were able to keep his favorite toy, so he will always be with us."

"Awww, poor Toby," said Donny. "That makes me sad."

"Me too," said Papa Steve. "I miss Toby, and so does Krug. He just mopes around most of the time. But he seems very happy to see you two, so that makes me extra glad you are here."

"I think you need to get another dog so Krug won't be so lonely," said Donny.

"Good idea, Donny," Grandma Cathy chimed in. "Papa and I have talked about that very thing."

"No dog could ever replace Toby," said Papa Steve sadly, "but we'll see."

Donny didn't like it when grown-ups said "We'll see," because it usually meant "No." *I will talk them into getting another a dog,* he thought to himself.

Krug got in the front seat by Grandma Cathy's feet and Mary Grace and Donny got in the back. Mary Grace turned her face to the window so Donny wouldn't see how sad she was. She wasn't even sure if it was because of Toby or because she missed home and her parents—or both.

Grandma Cathy leaned down and whispered to Krug that Mary Grace might like it if he climbed into the back and sat with her. Obediently, the dog got up, squeezed his way into the back, and lay down between the two children. Mary Grace could tell that Krug was as sad as she was, and gave his ears a nice long scratch.

"You and I are going to be friends," she said to the dog. "We both have something to be sad about."

Krug licked Mary Grace's hand, laid his head in her lap, and fell asleep. Soon, Donny laid his head on top of Krug's, and he fell asleep too.

Mary Grace gazed out the car window at the California landscape. Everything looked very different from Kansas, and she saw no reason to like it better. *I'll just have to get used to it,* she thought. *This is where we have to live for two whole years.* For Donny's sake, for Grandma and Papa's sake, and most of all, for her own sake, she tried to feel happy. It wasn't easy.

The drive from the airport to the ranch took almost three hours, including the bathroom-and-snacks break they took when they were halfway there. Krug and Donny slept through most of it while the other three chatted and listened to the radio. When they'd finally turned onto the long drive-way and passed through the gate, Papa Steve stopped the vehicle.

"Mary Grace, will you get out here with Krug so he can do his business? Be sure to keep him on his leash until the gate is closed though. When he's all done, the two of you can stretch your legs a little by walking up to the house. It's about a quarter mile."

"Sure, Papa," said Mary Grace. "Come on, Krugie—let's go for a walk."

"Wait'll you see that boy run," said Papa. "You might have trouble keeping up with him! He knows his dinner will be waiting when he gets up to the house."

"I'll be begging for my dinner too!" shouted Mary Grace, laughing as the car took off.

Papa Steve drove into the garage, and soon Krug was waiting by the kitchen door, wagging his tail. Mary Grace let him into the kitchen, and he went straight to his water bowl for a big, sloppy drink. When he'd drained the bowl, he looked up at Mary Grace and whimpered a little.

"Here you go, Krugie," she said and refilled it for him.

"Boy, does that dog love you," said Papa Steve. "I think you two can read each other's minds." Papa Steve was glad to see his dog so happy—and his granddaughter too.

"I think Krug wants me to fix him some dinner now," Mary Grace announced.

Papa Steve showed her where they kept his food and she filled up his bowl.

"Krug will be your friend forever now because that dog loves to eat," Papa Steve said.

When he'd wolfed down his dinner, Krug went over to Mary Grace and licked her hand.

"Look!" said Mary Grace. "Krug knows how to say *thank you* in dog."

"I'm hungry and want my dinner too," whined Donny, who had been watching the whole thing and feeling a little bit left out.

"Dinner will be ready very soon, Donny," said Grandma Cathy. "I just have to cook the spaghetti to go with the meatballs. Isn't that one of your favorites?"

"Yesss! Spageddy!"

"Kids, let's go get your bags and bring them in while your grandmother finishes making dinner," said Papa Steve.

Once again, he groaned when he tried to lift Donny's suitcase out of the trunk, and once again, Mary Grace helped him.

"It looks like all my marbles made it to California," said Donny with a big smile on his face.

After dinner, Grandma Cathy showed Mary Grace to her bedroom.

"This is a special room, child. It was your mother's from the time she was born until she left for college—and even after that, when she came home to visit. It looks a little different now, but when your mother was your age, these walls were covered with posters of all kinds of musical bands and movie stars."

"Really?" It was hard for Mary Grace to imagine her mom having crushes on movie stars or pop stars.

"Yes—but now it is *your* turn to decorate this room. I want you to feel free to put up anything you want on the walls. It is *your* room now to make exactly as you like it. I trust you."

"You do?"

"Of course, child. I'm sure you have very good taste."

"I won't put up anything crazy, I promise," said Mary Grace. She could not get the smile off her face as she looked around the bedroom. *Her* bedroom.

"Grandma, what was my mom like when she was my age?"

"She was a lot like *you*. She was smart. She was pretty. She was a good athlete too. She played soccer and rode horses. And, she was also very kind, like *you*. I see how sweet and patient you are with Donny and Krug, and with us grown-ups too. It was always your mom's kindness that made me most proud of her." She stopped talking and looked dreamy for a second, then continued. "I think that is why she married your father, Mary Grace—because he is such a kind person too. And, you want to know something? It doesn't surprise me one bit that they went off to Africa to help others in need. That is the kind of people they are."

Mary Grace thought about what her grandmother said and felt proud of her mom and dad.

"But . . . I still wish they hadn't gone," she said.

Papa Steve was the one to show Donny his bedroom.

"Here it is, kiddo," he said. "I think it will be a challenge to find somewhere in this room to keep all your marbles."

"I'll figure out where to put them," said Donny, smiling as he looked around. "My marbles are my favorite thing."

"There's something special you should know about this room, Donny."

"What's that, Papa?"

"This used to be my room when I was a boy."

That made Donny giggle.

"When were you a boy?" he asked.

"A long, long time ago," Papa Steve replied, laughing too.

"Was this your bed?"

"Nope. My old bed fell apart years ago. But you see all those books?" Papa Steve pointed to a large bookshelf overflowing with hardcovers and paperbacks in all shapes and sizes. "Those were mine—some from when I was as young as you."

"Do you have *Green Eggs and Ham?*"

"Hmmm . . . I know I *did* have it. Let's see if it's still here."

Papa Steve scanned the shelves until he spotted it.

"Here it is, Donny, right alongside a whole bunch of other books by Dr. Seuss."

"*Green Eggs and Ham* is my favorite book in the whole world!" exclaimed Donny.

"Well, how about we sit down and read it *right now*, then?"

"Yay! I know all the words!"

Papa Steve and Donny propped up the pillows on the bed and leaned back against them with the book open across their laps. By the time they finished reading it, it was Papa Steve's favorite book too.

CHAPTER
NINE

Tired out from their trip, Donny and Mary Grace went to bed early that night. Mary Grace thought for sure that she would fall asleep right away, but she was wrong. Eyes wide open in the dark, she lay in her new bed, staring at the ceiling for the longest time. Finally, she got up and headed toward the living room, where she heard voices.

"I thought you were tired," Papa Steve said when he saw her.

"I am, but I can't sleep."

"No problem, sweetheart," said Grandma Cathy. "Why don't you come over and sit with us by the fireplace?" She patted the sofa cushion next to her.

Mary Grace squeezed in between her grandparents. The heat from the fire warmed her feet.

"Isn't this nice? We can sit and talk. Here, put this blanket over you, dear. Now that winter is coming, it's starting to get chilly after the sun goes down. It never gets as cold here as it does in Kansas though."

"So," said Papa Steve, "we haven't seen you and Donny since the beginning of summer. We have a lot to catch up on."

"Oh, Papa! We've been talking to you on the phone every Sunday," said Mary Grace. "I'm pretty sure you know almost everything."

"Oh, I wouldn't say that. Not every little detail."

"I think I might be too tired to talk," said Mary Grace, "but I'm not too tired to listen." Turning to her grandma, she continued, "You know what I'd really like to hear about?"

"What's that, dear?"

"The Grandma Gang! Mom told me about how you have this group of friends called the Grandma Gang, and that you solved a mystery together!"

"Hoo-boy," said Papa Steve, "get ready to listen. That is definitely one of your grandmother's favorite stories to tell."

"Goody, because I love mysteries!"

Grandma Cathy pulled Mary Grace closer and said, "Where should I start?"

"At the beginning, of course," Mary Grace replied.

"Smart girl, Mary Grace," Papa Steve said with a smile.

"Well, let's see," said Grandma Cathy. "It all started with a phone call from my friend Lyndsey. She owns the 7-Eleven store just down the street from here. You know the one, right,

Mary Grace? It's where we always get Slurpees when you come to visit."

Mary Grace nodded, wanting her grandma to get on with the story.

"Well, anyway, Lyndsey called to tell me there had been another break-in at her store—the third one in three nights. All of the break-ins happened at night, after the store was closed, and the only thing stolen was candy."

"Candy?!" Mary Grace exclaimed curiously.

"Yes, candy," Grandma Cathy replied. "Of course, Lyndsey reported the break-ins to the sheriff's office, and some deputies came by and investigated, but they couldn't figure out who was responsible for the crimes. Lyndsey was naturally upset—who wouldn't be?—so she called me and asked if I would come talk to her about the situation. I said I would, but that I wanted to call some other friends to come along with me.

"The minute we hung up, I called La Shana Jackson and Elizabeth Blythe, who agreed to meet me at the 7-Eleven on our way to play bridge with your great-grandmother, Gigi. La Shana and Elizabeth are my oldest and dearest friends, stretching all the way back to when we worked at the court-house in Lompoc together. They were as curious as I was about Lyndsey's mysterious break-ins.

"When we got to the 7-Eleven, Lyndsey told us the whole story. It seemed that the burglars knew how to open the locked door at the back of the store. The first time they broke in, they must have been scared away before they took anything, because nothing was missing and they'd left the back door wide open, as if they'd left in a hurry. The second time they broke in, the only thing missing was candy and other snack food. Nothing else had been touched. The third time, they took snack food and candy again, but they also took all the eyeglasses and sunglasses from the rotating racks at the front of the store."

"It was probably kids, right?" said Mary Grace, the wheels in her head spinning at top speed.

"That's what the police thought," said Grandma Cathy, "but let me tell you the rest of the story. The sheriff's deputies played back the tapes from the store's security cameras and got a look at the burglars. There were two of them, and they were wearing baseball caps, hoodies, and raggedy jeans. The footage was too dark and blurry to see their faces, but—just like you—the deputies figured they were kids from the nearby high school. In the end, they dropped the investigation because they didn't have any more clues and there didn't seem to be a way to trace the stolen property."

"It probably all got eaten up!" Mary Grace said, laughing. "So, how did the Grandma Gang solve the mystery?"

"With our noggins, that's how! We ladies figured it out and caught the burglars!" Grandma Cathy said proudly. "And it was actually the newspapers that called La Shana, Elizabeth, and me the 'Grandma Gang,' and we all kind of liked that."

"That's so cool!" said Mary Grace. "But *how* did you figure it out?"

"Patience, child, and let me finish the story. When we asked Lyndsey for more details, she told us that what was missing didn't make much sense. Most of her candy and snack racks were cleaned out, but the burglars were kind of picky and left whole bins untouched. They took every single Hostess Cupcake, Ho Ho, and Twinkie, along with all the donuts and cinnamon rolls. Lyndsey also told us that the burglars even seemed to have favorite candy bars. They took all the Mars bars and Three Musketeers, but they left the Snickers and PayDays alone."

"That's weird. I love Snickers and PayDays," Mary Grace interjected.

"Me too, Mary Grace," said Papa Steve, who had been listening quietly to a story he had heard many times before.

"Stop, you two, before I forget where I was," said Grandma Cathy. "Anyway . . . with that clue, it didn't take us long to solve the mystery of the persnickety burglars. 'It sounds like the burglars have the same taste as my mother, Gigi,' I told my friends—and they looked at each other and laughed.

"'We'd better warn your mom she's about to get arrested,' joked La Shana—but we all knew that Gigi would never really do such a thing.

"'You know,' said Elizabeth, 'these burglars picked all of the easy-to-eat snacks. Nothing too chewy and nothing with nuts.'"

"Yes!" said Mary Grace. "PayDays and Snickers have both nuts *and* caramel. That's why I like them!"

"After we all thought about this for a minute or two," Grandma Cathy continued, "La Shana smacked her forehead and said, 'You know what? I'll bet you next week's grocery money that whoever stole this stuff has false teeth, like my Aunt Ruth. She won't go near anything too chewy or crunchy for fear it might dislodge her dentures!'

"'That sure doesn't sound like high school kids to me,' Elizabeth said. 'They'll eat everything and anything—even the ones with braces! And you know what else? None of the teenagers in my karate classes have false teeth. A lot of my karate students have braces, and I see them eat hard candy, nuts, and chewy candy all the time.'

"Elizabeth also quickly realized that there was a home for senior citizens a few blocks away, right next door to her karate studio—and only two blocks from Lyndsey's 7-Eleven store.

"'I bet some of those seniors have false teeth,' said Lyndsey, 'or at least weak teeth and jaws.'

"Well, Lyndsey was skeptical. 'But what about what they were wearing?' she asked us just as we were congratulating ourselves for being such smart old birds. 'They sure weren't dressed like older people.' To which I replied that one of the things you learn working around the courthouse is that people can't be identified by their clothes—not if they don't want to be."

"Wow, Grandma," said Mary Grace, clearly impressed. "That was very good mystery-solving! What happened next?"

"Hold your horses, Mary Grace," said Papa Steve. "Your grandmother will get to the point eventually."

"Oh, come on, you two!" said Grandma Cathy. "Give me a chance to catch my breath. Anyway, Lyndsey started to see things the way we did and called the sheriff's office to tell them what we'd figured out to confirm that it was possible that the burglars on the security video could have been old people, dressed up like teenagers with hoodies and baseball caps so you couldn't see their faces. The deputy agreed that it was possible, but to be careful when making assumptions.

"We were sure we were right, and we wanted to prove it—so we did something that probably wasn't very sensible.

"The next night, with Lyndsey's permission, we three hid out in the store after it closed. At about midnight, we heard noises out back, and we crouched down behind the counter. From there, we saw the knob on the back door rotate and the door open. We kept real still while two people carrying large shopping bags made a beeline for the Hostess Cupcakes and Twinkies rack! They tossed all the cakes into their bags real quick, then headed for the candy aisle.

"At that point, just like we planned it, La Shana, Elizabeth, and I jumped up from behind the counter and yelled, 'WHO ARE YOU? WHAT ARE YOU DOING?' I don't mind telling you, child, my heart was beating so hard, I thought my chest might burst open!

"The two burglars jumped a mile when we shouted, and headed for the back door, but Elizabeth beat 'em to it—she's pretty fast on her feet. She blocked the door and put her hands up in her best karate position. 'I'm a black belt,' she shouted, 'and you don't want to mess with me!' Honestly, I don't know where she gets her courage. I guess maybe it's from all those self-defense classes and such—"

"Grandma!" said Mary Grace impatiently. "What happened after that?!"

"Why . . . they dropped their bags and gave up," Grandma Cathy said. "And when they pulled off their caps and big sunglasses, we could see they were two older folks, like us—a man and a lady."

"What happened to them? Did they get in trouble?" Mary Grace asked.

"Oh, yes. We told them to stay put, and Elizabeth called the sheriff's office. In a few minutes, that same deputy who'd been so snippy with us came to the store and said he was going to arrest them and take them to the station. He thanked us for catching them, but he was a little mad at us for meddling in police work and putting ourselves in a dangerous situation."

"But why did those people rob the store, Grandma? Were they too old and senile to know what they were doing?"

"No, it wasn't that, honey. Honestly, I think they were just craving some snacks. They knew what they were doing was wrong, but all they ever got to eat at the senior home was meat and potatoes and such. When they asked for sweets or treats, the people in charge told them candy and cakes weren't good for them. But, you know ... everybody needs a treat once in a while."

"That seems kind of mean," said Mary Grace, instantly feeling sorry for the seniors.

"Yes, it does, Mary Grace. We all thought so too. Anyway, there we stood—the deputies, and us, and the candy burglars.

"'We know stealing is wrong,' said the lady. 'We did a crazy thing, and we're sorry about it. If you just let us go, we'll never break the law again.' Well, the deputies looked at us, and we looked at the burglars.

"'We can't give the candy back,' said the man. 'I'm afraid that's long gone. But all of those glasses we took for our friends? We can give all of those back.'

"'Come on, officers, I said. Seems like they didn't really do much harm. I'm sure our friend Lyndsey will be happy with just an apology.'

"In the end, the deputies talked it over with their bosses, and everybody agreed that if they gave back the glasses, along with some money to cover the cost of the sweets, and performed some community service, they wouldn't have to face charges. Of course, they would have to apologize to Lyndsey and promise never to take anything again."

"That seems fair," said Mary Grace, "but I still think they should all get some candy once in a while."

"You and Lyndsey think exactly alike, Mary Grace," chimed in Papa Steve. "Let your grandma tell you what happened next."

"Well," said Grandma Cathy, "we told Lyndsey all about the burglars and why they kept breaking into her store, and you know what she did? She marched right over to the senior center and talked to the people in charge there. She told them older people need treats once in a while, just as much as kids do. And she offered to come by the home once a week and sell candy and cakes to any of the seniors who wanted them. And that is exactly what she does now—every single Monday afternoon."

"And that was the end of the story?" asked Mary Grace.

"Well . . . not quite. The deputies felt like they better pay a visit to the senior home too, just to tell everybody over there that they'd be keeping a sharp eye out for any lawbreakers. Whether you're young or old, you can't be breaking into people's stores and taking what you want. I think they all learned their lesson. Those two burglars were really just good people who had made a big mistake.

"Anyway, we figured that was the end of it—but some reporter got wind of the story and thought it belonged in the newspaper. He came to the 7-Eleven to interview Lyndsey and the three of us. I sent your mom and dad the clipping of the article he wrote, with our pictures and everything. The headline read, 'Senior Burglars Are No Match for the

Grandma Gang.' That's how we got our name, and that's what everybody calls us now."

"Wow!" said Mary Grace. "You guys are famous!"

"Well . . . maybe to our friends and family," Grandma said, laughing. "And you know, it all made us realize how lucky we are to be healthy and busy and have one another to do things with. So now, La Shana, Elizabeth, and I go over to the senior home for a visit each week after bridge. They look forward to it—especially Kevin and Dolly, the two old burglars. They are just as sweet as pie—can you believe it?"

"That's so cool, Grandma! Maybe I can go with you to visit them sometime."

"It's quite a story, isn't it?" said Papa Steve, giving Grandma Cathy a peck on the cheek. "And you know what? Since then, the sheriff's office calls your grandma and her pals once in a while when they are stumped and need help figuring out a mystery."

"Really?!" Now Mary Grace was genuinely excited. "Grandma," she asked, "do you think that maybe I could be a member of the Grandma Gang too and help you solve crimes? Dad always says I'm good at figuring things out—and it's my favorite thing to do!"

"We'll see, sweetheart. But right now, this grandma and grandpa and this smart little girl all need to get some rest!"

Mary Grace climbed back into bed, her head spinning with the story her grandma had told her. She couldn't wait to tell her mom what she'd learned—but she figured it might be too late to call Kansas. Instead, she just sent a quick text:

> I heard the Grandma Gang story tonight. So cool.
> I miss you guys. I miss Kansas.

CHAPTER

TEN

The first day in California was a good one. The flight was a lot of fun. Grandma Cathy and Papa Steve are so nice. Krug loves me. This might not be so bad. Only two more years to go. 364 days plus 365 days. That's . . . 729 days?! OMG!

Mary Grace had been feeling happy upon awakening, and had remained that way until she did the math. She should not have added up all those days. There were so many of them that it made her feel sad again.

Today was Friday, the day Grandma Cathy had said she was going to take Mary Grace and Donny to their new school to register. They'd be starting classes on Monday morning and were both eager to see what the place was like.

Still in her pajamas, Mary Grace walked into the kitchen to find Grandma Cathy cooking breakfast and Donny helping her.

"Grandma asked me to break the eggs," Donny said proudly from his perch at the kitchen table. "I have to break eight eggs and put them in this bowl."

"Do a good job for Grandma Cathy, buddy," said Mary Grace, figuring there would be a bit of cleaning up to do before they could sit down to eat.

"After you break the eggs, you can make the pancake mix for me, Donny," said Grandma Cathy over her shoulder as she cooked the bacon.

"Uh-oh, Grandma, I hope you have a big cleaning crew coming in soon," Mary Grace joked.

"Why, yes I do, and she just walked into the kitchen in her PJs!" said Grandma Cathy before adding, "Oh, I'm just teasing you. I don't mind a little mess if Donny is having fun helping me out."

Mary Grace could see that Donny was indeed having fun. He was cracking the eggs with such intense concentration that his tongue poked out of the corner of his mouth. After each one, he would sit back and smile.

"On second thought," said Grandma, "maybe you do want to help Donny with the pancake mix. Flour can be pretty tricky to clean up."

Breakfast was delicious, and cleanup took just a little while with Papa Steve pitching in to help.

"Has anyone fed Krug yet?" he asked. "Seemed like he was eyeing our food and feeling sorry for himself."

When he heard his name, Krug got to his feet from where he was lying in the corner of the kitchen, padded over to Mary Grace, and wagged his tail.

"Oh! I thought somebody else did it," said Mary Grace.

"That's okay, honey," said Papa, "but you know what? I think we'll make the morning feeding your job—how about it? Krug loves you already. In fact, I haven't seen that pup so happy in ages. He latched right onto you like you're his best friend for life! You seem to know how to speak 'dog.' Are you some kind of dog whisperer?"

"Ha! Maybe I am," Mary Grace replied proudly. "I'd love to feed Krug . . . since he and I have so much in common."

She didn't elaborate, and her grandparents decided to leave it at that.

After Mary Grace fed Krug and got dressed, everyone took a walk down to the pond.

"Look, look! The ducks are here," Donny squealed.

"They must have known you were coming, Donny," said Grandma Cathy.

"How did they know?"

"Maybe they saw our airplane," said Mary Grace.

"They look hungry," said Papa Steve, pulling a baggie full of breadcrumbs from his pocket. "Maybe you should feed them."

While Donny and Mary Grace took turns tossing crumbs to the ducks, the grown-ups sat down on a couple of Adirondack chairs close to the water's edge and watched.

When the breadcrumbs were gone, Papa Steve said, "Hey, you two—how about a little fishing?"

"Yes!" shouted Donny.

Papa Steve ducked into the little shed near the pond and grabbed a couple of fishing rods and life jackets.

"Remember, kiddos, safety first . . . especially near water," Papa Steve said as he slipped a life jacket over the head of each of the kids and then put one on himself.

For the next hour, he patiently helped them bait their hooks and taught them a little about casting. He'd prepared for their visit by asking one of the ranch workers to stock the pond with fish the week before, so it was a sure bet his grandkids would have a successful time of it—and they did! Everybody had lots of fun snagging fish, reeling them in, and learning how to gently place the smaller ones back in the pond so they could grow a little bigger.

"These big boys will make a wonderful dinner," said Grandma Cathy, admiring their catch. "When we get back, I'm going to show you how I take the bones out!"

Grandma Cathy had worked with Mrs. Miller ahead of time to make sure Mary Grace and Donny could register in the California school system, and when she arrived with the kids for their first visit, everything was in order. North Elementary School had let out early on this particular Friday for teacher workshops and parent–teacher conferences, so it was a good time for Donny and Mary Grace to get a look at their new classrooms.

First, they met the school principal, Mrs. Stuart, and Mary Grace peppered her with questions, especially ones revolving around Donny.

"What are Donny's classes going to be like, Mrs. Stuart?" she asked. "Donny needs extra help." Mary Grace was more concerned about Donny and his classes than her own. She asked many questions about North Elementary School and special classes for kids with Down syndrome.

"It is very kind of you to worry about your brother, Mary Grace," said the principal, who was very impressed with how Mary Grace interacted with and cared for her brother.

"Donny will be in Classroom Five, which is a classroom for children with special needs. His teacher will be Mrs.

Hagen. She is one of the best teachers in the school, and has been trained to teach children like Donny. She loves her students, and they love her right back!"

"That sounds perfect," said Mary Grace. "Doesn't it, Donny?"

"I love North Elementary School," said Donny.

"Maybe you are wondering about your own teacher, Mary Grace," said Mrs. Stuart. "Her name is Ms. Root, and she is a great teacher too! All the kids want to be in her class, which is in Classroom Twenty-Five."

"Do I get to meet her today?" asked Mary Grace, who was getting pretty excited about her new school.

"Yes, I think Ms. Root and Mrs. Hagen are both still in their classrooms, if you two would like to meet them."

"Me first! This is the new best day of my life," said Donny, with his usual enthusiasm.

"Okay, Donny," said Mrs. Stuart, "let's head over to Room Five now."

Donny's big "YESSSS!" made Mary Grace and Grandma Cathy laugh.

"I wish I could be happy all the time, like Donny," said his big sister.

When they met Mrs. Hagen, Mary Grace immediately knew that Donny would be happy in her class. Sure enough, teacher and student shared a big hug when it was time to leave her room.

Ms. Root was young and full of energy. Mary Grace liked her right away, and even more when she began talking about all of the fun things they'd be learning in science.

"We will see you both on Monday," said Mrs. Stuart as they walked back down the hall toward the front door.

"I can't wait!" Donny announced.

"Same here!" said Mary Grace, surprising herself by how happy she felt at that moment.

When they got home, Papa Steve was waiting for them, happy to see big smiles on their faces.

"I guess this has been a nice, busy day," he said. "Instead of getting hot and smelly cooking up fish, how about we all go out to Friendly's for dinner?"

"What a great idea!" Grandma Cathy said. "I think Donny will love their hamburgers. And afterward, we can go see Mom." Turning to the children, she added, "Your great-grandma Gigi is very eager to see both of you. You remember her, right?"

"Of course we do," said Mary Grace. "How could I ever forget the woman I was named after? She is the only other *Mary Grace* I have ever met."

"Donny," said Grandma Cathy, "maybe your good buddy Ed will be there too."

"Yay!" said Donny. "Ed likes marbles, just like me. I am going to bring my favorite ones to show him."

"Okay, sport," said Papa Steve, "but not too many!"

Donny ran up to his room. He had moved his entire marble collection to a box on the floor of his closet. He dug both hands into the box, searching for his best aggies, glassies, and cat's-eyes. He put ten of his favorite marbles in his pocket, just in case he got to meet Ed at Gigi's condo. He would love to get a chance to show him his best marbles. As he closed his closet door, Donny decided the box was a much better place for his marbles than the floor, which is where he was planning to keep them before finding the box. He was glad that the box kept the marbles from rolling all over.

"We are going to take you to a new place that makes great hamburgers," announced Papa Steve when Donny came back into the room, "I know Donny loves hamburgers, and I do too."

"Yeah! Let's go!" Donny was ready.

"On our way, let's go down to the pond again and see if the ducks are back," said Papa Steve as they hurried out the door.

Gigi couldn't stop smiling when she saw Donny and Mary Grace. "You have both grown so much since last time I saw you!" she said.

Donny nodded and stood proudly on his tiptoes.

"Can I meet Ed tonight, the boy with the marble collection?" he asked his great-grandma. "I brought my best marbles to show him. I couldn't bring all of them because they are too heavy!"

"Of course, Donny. I asked Ed to stop by especially to meet you. But he isn't a boy; he's almost an adult. He helps his mother and all the other people who live here. You know, Donny . . . Ed went to school in a special classroom just like you do."

"He did? Did he have Mrs. Hagen? She's going to be my teacher, and she is really nice!"

"You can ask him all about it when he gets here, Donny. He is a very nice man. He helps everyone who lives here with their wheelchairs and walkers. He helps them move heavy things and carry their grocery bags. I don't think we could get along without him. As soon as he gets here, we're going to have some nice tea and cookies."

"Can we have *milk* and cookies?" asked Donny. "I don't think I like tea. Do I like tea, Mary Grace?" Donny asked his sister.

"No, I don't think you do—but I know you like cookies!" replied Mary Grace.

"Yes! Especially Snickerdoodles!"

Ding-dong!

"Donny, why don't you answer the door?" said Gigi.

When Donny opened it, there stood Ed and his mother, Mrs. Knight.

"Come on in," called out Gigi.

"You're Ed!" said Donny as they walked into the living room. He then proceeded to pull all the marbles from his two pockets.

"Wow, your marbles are beautiful," said Ed. "Can I hold them?"

Donny placed all of the marbles into Ed's big hands, and Ed looked closely at each one before handing it back.

"These are really cool, Donny!" said Ed. Then he turned to his mom and said, "Can I take Donny to our house to show him my marbles?"

"But we just got here, Ed," Mrs. Knight replied, and I think Gigi has some cookies especially for us.

"But . . . can I? Please? Just for a few minutes?" Ed was very excited to find someone who liked marbles as much as he did.

"Let them go while I get the tea and cookies ready," Gigi said. "Mary Grace, why don't you go along too?"

"Okay, you three," said Mrs. Knight. "Go on . . . but come back in a few minutes, or we'll eat up all the cookies!"

Ed took Mary Grace and Donny to the Knights' condo and unlocked the door with the key that hung from a lanyard around his neck.

"Come to my room, you guys," he said. "My mother makes me keep my marbles in there because people could trip on them if they were all around the condo."

Ed's marble collection was even bigger than Donny's, which Mary Grace hadn't thought was possible. While the two boys chattered away about the different colors and kinds of marbles, Mary Grace looked out the window. She wasn't all that interested in marbles, but she was happy to see Donny having a good time.

After about ten minutes, she said, "Sorry to interrupt but I think we better go back before the cookies are gone."

"Okay, but you guys have to come back another time," said Ed, cleaning up all the marbles from the floor. Donny noticed that he kept them in old coffee cans and wondered if Grandma Cathy had some old cans he could use for his marbles.

When they got back to Gigi's condo, the grown-ups were talking and not paying any attention at all to the cookies, which were sitting on a pretty plate on the coffee table, along with a pitcher of milk and a pot of tea. While the boys told everybody about their marbles, Mary Grace poured big glasses of milk for Donny and Ed, and a cup of tea for herself—with lots of sugar.

"So, Mary Grace," said Gigi, "I've been hearing all about your parents and their new adventure."

"Yes," said Mary Grace proudly. "We all hated to leave Wichita, but Mom and Dad had to go do very important work in Africa, so we came to California for a while." It was the first time she had thought about her parents and their trip without feeling sad and angry.

The evening passed by quickly. While Donny and Ed talked more about their marble collections and school and other favorite things, Mary Grace and the adults talked about Wichita and California and all of the great things to do in both places. When Gigi told her how lucky she was to be living on a ranch with all those animals and lots of places to play, she thought, *I guess, maybe, I really am lucky.*

As they were leaving, Gigi said, "I hope you kids will come visit me as often as you can."

"As long as I can go see Ed's marbles again, I'll come!" said Donny, and everybody laughed. "And ... Grandma," he added, "do you have any old coffee cans? Ed keeps his marbles in coffee cans, and I want to do the same thing. Cans are better than boxes!"

"I'll look for some tomorrow, Donny," Grandma Cathy replied. "I'm sure we have some stashed away somewhere."

Mary Grace smiled all the way home and thought to herself that living with Grandma Cathy and Papa Steve in California might not be as awful as she'd thought.

CHAPTER

ELEVEN

M ary Grace woke up with Donny's face about eighteen inches from hers. She could feel his breath . . . and smell it. He hadn't brushed his teeth yet—yuck.

"I've been waiting for you to open your eyes, Mary Grace!" he said. "I've been waiting a *really* long time."

"Ugh . . . go back to sleep, Donny," she replied and pulled the covers over her head.

"No! Today is Monday and it's time to wake up for our first day of school!"

Donny's teacher, Mrs. Hagen, welcomed him to his classroom the minute Mary Grace dropped him off, and then introduced him to all the other children. He had such a good time all morning that when the final bell rang, he couldn't believe his first day was over already.

At home after school, he told his grandma, grandpa, and sister all about it.

"There were so many fun things to do," he said, "and all these games to play! And Mrs. Hagen treated me like I was super special. She told everybody in the class that she was making up a new thing called Donny's Friend of the Week. It's a treat for whoever gets chosen, and that person is my special friend all week long, and goes with me to recess and lunch, and waits for me outside of the bathroom, and helps me learn all the rules of the class. This week, my Friend of the Week is a girl named Keisha, and she's pretty!"

"That's wonderful, Donny! I'm so glad you are settling in at school," said Grandma Cathy. "How about you, Mary Grace? How was your first day?"

Mary Grace had a scowl on her face. She did *not* love her first day of school, the way Donny did.

"Ms. Root was nice, and the class was interesting," she said, "but . . . I felt like an oddball. I mean, everybody else has been in that class for two months already—and most of them knew each other even before that. They're already all friends and I'm, like, the new weirdo kid with no friends at all. In Wichita, I had lots of friends." She put her chin down on the kitchen table in a sulk.

"Oh, sweetheart . . . it's only been one day," said Grandma Cathy in that soothing voice grown-ups use when they want to make kids feel better. "You might have to be a little patient with the other children. Making friends takes a little time, but I'm sure that soon they will all like you as much as your friends in Wichita do."

"I don't know why Mom and Dad had to go to Africa!" Mary Grace replied, her voice trembling a little bit, like she might start crying.

"Don't feel bad, Mary Grace!" said Donny. "I'm your best friend, remember?"

In spite of her mood, Mary Grace smiled at her brother and ruffled his hair.

"Why don't you go play in your room for a little while, Donny?" said Grandma Cathy. And pick out a book for us to read later, before bed."

When Donny had scampered off to his room, Grandma Cathy turned back to Mary Grace and said, "Well, Papa and I are glad you are here, that's for sure—and Krug is overjoyed." Right at that moment, Krug had his head on Mary Grace's lap and looked blissful as she scratched his head and neck. "You know," Grandma Cathy continued, "if you are feeling lonely for your friends in Wichita, you can always write them letters. I'm sure they'll write you back."

"Oh, Grandma, kids don't write letters anymore. I've been texting with my friends back home *a lot*, but it isn't the same as being there." She didn't tell her grandma what she had written in her texts because she didn't want to hurt her feelings.

"I see! Well, that's nice and quick, isn't it? But I guess I'm a little old-fashioned. I still love getting a letter in the mail, opening the envelope, and reading it. I don't think I'll ever get used to emails and texting. How about your parents, then? They are probably settled down in their village by now. You could send them a letter and include some pictures of you and Donny here at the ranch."

"I told you, Grandma, I can just send a *text* or an *email* and *attach* the photos."

"Ah, well. Whatever makes you happy, I suppose." She looked dreamy for a second, then perked up and said, "Oh! I nearly forgot. I bought a little something for you today to celebrate your first day of school. Wait here."

She left the kitchen and returned a minute later with a gift bag.

Mary Grace moved the tissue paper aside and pulled out a T-shirt that read, "I ♥ my dog."

"Thanks, Grandma—I love it," she said, and pulled it on right over what she was wearing.

"Aw, it looks great on you," said Grandma Cathy. "Let's take a picture right now of you and Krug so you can send it to your parents."

"Okay, but wait! I have an idea." Mary Grace ran to her bedroom and got the "I love California" T-shirt out of her drawer.

"Let's put this on Krugie," she said when she returned, and they wriggled him into it.

"I'll take it with your phone," said Grandma Cathy. "Your mom and dad are going to love it. Now, smile!"

Mary Grace put on the best smile she could manage. She then sent the picture off to her parents—along with a note, which she didn't share with Grandma Cathy:

> Krug loves California—because he has never been to Kansas.

> Please come back to Kansas so Donny and I can come home.

After dinner that evening, Mary Grace again settled by the fire with her grandma, while Papa Steve played the marble and dominoes game with Donny in the bedroom.

"So, Mary Grace," said Grandma Cathy, "did you hear how Mrs. Hagen assigned Donny a 'Friend of the Week'? That was very thoughtful. Maybe we could do something special for Mrs. Hagen and Donny's new friend."

"How about if I ask Mrs. Hagen if I can bring cupcakes to Donny's class for everyone to share since they are being so nice to him?" asked Mary Grace.

"Good idea, love!"

"I wish Ms. Root would assign a 'Friend of the Week' for *me*," Mary Grace said wistfully.

Grandma Cathy just smiled. She understood that if Mary Grace was a little bit patient, she'd settle into North Elementary School just fine.

Ms. Root must have noticed that Mary Grace seemed unhappy on her first day and had gone to recess and lunch all by herself. She decided to do something. It was actually similar to Donny's Friend of the Week. Sometimes it seemed like Ms. Root could read her students' minds.

Ms. Root decided to ask one of the other girls, Penelope Li, to help Mary Grace find her away around and get settled.

"Sure, Ms. Root," Penelope replied. "I'll help her out. I'll invite her to have lunch with me and my friends tomorrow."

The teacher hoped the two girls would become good friends. She understood how hard it was to be the "new girl," and Penelope understood it too. She'd been born in China and had come to the United States with her parents just before she'd started third grade at North Elementary School. At home, she spoke both English and Mandarin, but Ms. Root knew she had kept that a secret from her school friends. All she'd really wanted was to fit in—and by the time she got to Ms. Root's fifth-grade class, her English was as good as everyone else's, if not better.

Penelope kept her word and asked Mary Grace to eat lunch at her usual table. Mary Grace was too polite to say no, but the truth was, she didn't fully trust Penelope's offer of friendship. *She's only being nice to me because Ms. Root told her to,* she thought—because Mary Grace was good at figuring things out. But after several days of hanging out with Penelope and her friends, Mary Grace felt a little more confident. *Maybe Penelope actually likes me,* she thought, and hoped she was right because she desperately wanted a friend.

"Hey, Penelope," she said toward the end of her first week, "want to help me with something? I promise it'll be fun."

"What?"

"I'm throwing a cupcake party for the special ed class."

"Wow, that's really nice of you."

"Well, you know . . . I told you my brother Donny is in that class, and the other kids and teacher have been really nice to him. It made me want to do something special for them."

"So what do you need me to do?"

"Nothing, really—my grandma and I already made the cupcakes. All you have to do is come with me and make sure all the kids are having fun. And eat some cupcakes, of course!"

"Sounds good to me."

Mary Grace told Penelope that Mrs. Hagen had suggested she bring some sugar-free and gluten-free treats along with the regular cupcakes, for the kids who had allergies.

Her grandma had helped her make a big batch of chocolate cupcakes, and they were going to stop at a special bakery for the rest.

The party was on Friday, and Mary Grace and Penelope were excused from class an hour early for it. Grandma Cathy had been invited too, and it was a good thing she was there, because kids who are full of sugar can get pretty loud and jumpy.

At a certain point, Mrs. Hagen said, "Okay, everyone, no more cupcakes!" and sent the extra ones to the teacher's lounge, figuring the grown-ups would appreciate them as much as the kids did on a Friday afternoon.

Penelope and Mary Grace had so much fun at the party together that they became real friends then and there. Penelope confided in Mary Grace that her family was from China, and that she often spoke Mandarin at home.

"Wow," said Mary Grace, "I wish I could speak another language! Especially Chinese. It has its own alphabet and everything!"

"Yeah . . . it's cool, I guess," said Penelope, "but I sort of like to keep all that private so nobody thinks I'm weird or something."

"Don't worry; I know how to keep secrets with my friends," said Mary Grace.

"Let's pinky swear," said Penelope, and they locked their little fingers together and shook them up and down.

After that, Penelope and Mary Grace spent almost all their recess and lunch time together, and soon another girl, Tiffany Johnson, began to hang out with them as well. Mary Grace hoped that Tiffany would be her second-best friend, but Tiffany didn't seem as interested in her as Penelope did.

One day a couple of weeks later, Donny and Papa Steve were out in the orchard with Krug, but Mary Grace was moping around the house, looking sadder than usual.

It's a beautiful day, dear," said Grandma Cathy. "Don't you want to spend some time outside with Donny and Papa?"

"I don't really feel like it, Grandma," Mary Grace replied, then turned her face away and looked out the living room window.

"Hmm, well why don't we have a little chat then? Run to the kitchen, and grab us a couple of nice, cold Diet Cokes, will you?"

Mary Grace did as she was asked, bringing a couple of napkins too so they wouldn't make rings on the table. She set one of the Diet Cokes on a napkin in front of her grandma. She popped open the other one and settled into her favorite comfy chair near the fireplace.

The two sat in silence for a few minutes, and then Mary Grace said, "I have a problem at school."

Grandma Cathy just tilted her head and waited patiently. She was a very good listener, especially when somebody had a problem.

"So. . ." Mary Grace began, "I already told you I had a little trouble figuring out school at first. I felt left out and stuff. But then I met Penelope and everything got better. We started hanging out a lot and having lunch together, and then Penelope's friend Tiffany started eating with us too. Which is fine, except . . . sometimes I think Tiffany is jealous. Like, she wants to have Penelope all to herself and wants me to just go away."

"I see," said Grandma Cathy. "That sounds a little uncomfortable, but I have a feeling it will work itself out. Especially if Penelope is as good a friend as she seems to be."

"I . . . guess so. But that isn't even my biggest problem. There's something else. I wasn't going to tell anybody because I like to figure things out by myself, but . . . it's really bothering me." Mary Grace paused, took a deep breath, then started speaking very quickly: "After morning recess today, I found a note in my desk. At first, I figured it was from Penelope, but then I read it, and, well, I couldn't believe what it said, so I— It said . . ." Mary Grace had to stop speaking because she had a lump in her throat. She swiped at the tears in her eyes with the back of her hand, then reached into her pocket and pulled out a folded piece of notebook paper. "Here, Grandma," she said. "Read it yourself."

Scrawled in purple Sharpie ink was written the following:

Your brother Donny is a retard.

You and Donny need to go back where you
came from.

"Oh, my," was all Grandma Cathy could say. She was shocked.

"I know! Who would write such a terrible thing about Donny? And *me?* Why do they want to hurt us both?" The tears Mary Grace had been trying to hold back broke free, and she sobbed into the napkin she'd brought for herself. When she'd blown her nose and settled back in her chair, she said, "The funny part is that I really *want* to go back to Kansas! If only this mean person knew that, maybe they would leave me alone!"

"Oh, honey . . . did you show the note to Ms. Root?"

"No, and I didn't tell Penelope about it either. I guess I didn't want to make a big deal out of it or seem like a crybaby."

"But, it *is* a big deal, Mary Grace. It's bullying, and that is a very serious matter," Grandma Cathy said, emphasizing the word *bullying.*

Bullying? Mary Grace had heard of it, but she'd always pictured it differently.

"But Grandma," she said, "isn't bullying like when a big kid beats up a smaller one on the playground or something? This was just a *note.*"

"Make no mistake, Mary Grace, this is bullying, plain and simple, and we need to put a stop to it."

Mary Grace thought her grandma sounded like a lawyer, which is exactly what she used to do for a living.

"But Grandma," she pleaded, "I don't want the other kids in the class to know about it. They'll think I'm a tattletale, and then everybody will hate me, instead of just this one person."

Grandma Cathy looked serious.

"I know social matters at school can be tricky, honey, but we can't just leave this alone, which is why I'm very glad you told me about it. That was the right thing to do."

"Okay, but I don't want to make a big deal out of it. Trust me, if I do that, I will never have any friends as long as I live in California—which is a really long time!" She wiped her nose again, then added, "Maybe if I just pretend it never happened—like I didn't get the note—that will be the end of it."

"I understand your feelings, honey, but this is a matter to be discussed with Ms. Root. In fact, I think you should call her right now. She gave us her number, remember?"

"I . . . I don't want to call her, Grandma. Could *you*, maybe, do it?"

"Of course I can, sweetheart. I promise I won't make too big a deal out of it, okay? But your teacher can help us figure out what to do next."

Grandma Cathy went into the kitchen and grabbed her cell phone, then came back to the living room with it. She scrolled through her saved numbers until she found the one Ms. Root had given her, and pressed the button to make the call. When Ms. Root answered, they talked for a minute, and then Grandma Cathy read her the note.

"Please understand that Mary Grace would like this handled carefully," she added. "She is concerned that the class won't react well to a 'tattletale.' Do you think maybe you and Mrs. Hagen could meet with Mary Grace and me to talk about it?"

"That is exactly what I was going to suggest," said Ms. Root. "How about tomorrow after school? This is a serious matter, and I'm glad you called me about it."

Mary Grace had been doing her best to follow the conversation, but could only hear her grandma's side of it.

"What did she say?" she asked as soon as Grandma Cathy put down the phone.

"Just as I figured, honey, she takes this very seriously. We're going to have a meeting with her and Donny's teacher tomorrow after school. I think Mrs. Stuart may join us as well."

Mary Grace didn't say anything, but her mouth turned downward in a frown. Had she been wrong to tell her grandma about the note?

I just know the whole class will think I'm a loser now, she thought to herself.

She didn't mention anything about the note to her parents in her daily email to them. Why make them worry when they're so far away, she figured. It isn't like they could help all the way from Africa. And anyway, she didn't want them thinking their daughter was a *loser*.

CHAPTER
TWELVE

"I am appalled that any child at North Elementary School would use that word." That's how Mrs. Stuart began the meeting the next afternoon. "That 'R' word—I can't even bring myself to say it—is simply unacceptable in this day and age, and cannot be tolerated in a school such as ours, which values our students' differences so highly." Mrs. Stuart looked at each one of the faces in front of her and then went on, "But this is not just about a word. Telling Mary Grace and Donny to 'go back where they came from' is so inhospitable that I would consider it a form of bullying. And bullying will *not* be permitted in our school. Mrs. Hagen, as the teacher of our beautiful Room Five students, would you like to share your thoughts?"

Mrs. Hagen cleared her throat and said, "Well . . . let me start by saying I am grateful that Donny and his classmates don't know about the note. They are lovely, sensitive children whose feelings are easily hurt. For that reason, I'd like to keep this conversation among the people in this room."

"I agree," said Grandma Cathy. "I know that Mary Grace would like this to stay private. She does not want all the students to know about it. We are keeping it a secret from Donny at home. Let's try to keep this news quiet. Mary Grace and Donny are the victims here. We must protect them."

Mary Grace sat next to Grandma Cathy with an envelope in front of her on the table.

"My Grandma is right," said Mary Grace. "I just want this to all go away. I don't want all the kids to know. It's already tough enough to be the new kid in school. I don't want to be more of an oddball or have it get any worse. I just don't want all this." Tears welled in her eyes.

"Of course, Mary Grace," said the principal. "I understand how you feel. You've done nothing wrong and do not deserve to be singled out in any way. Let's keep the whole situation from getting any worse, shall we?"

"Mrs. Stuart," interjected Ms. Root, "I am sorry to say that it has already gotten worse. Mary Grace, please show Mrs. Stuart what you found in your desk today."

Without a word, Mary Grace pushed the envelope in Mrs. Stuart's direction. It had her first name scrawled on it in purple Sharpie.

When Mrs. Stuart read the note, her eyes grew wide.

"Oh, my heavens," she said. This *is* worse—much worse. This is a threat. This is beyond bullying. This has got to be stopped. The school district has a zero-tolerance policy when it comes to bullying and threats. Rather than read this aloud, I'd like to pass it around so you can each see it for yourself."

The note was passed around the room as tears rolled down Mary Grace's cheeks.

> Snitches get stitches so you better keep your mouth shut.

> You will get hurt if you tell the teacher or anyone else about this.

> Your brother is still a retard.

"At this point," continued Mrs. Stuart, "I will need to consult with the school board about how to proceed. Thank you, everyone, for gathering today, and rest assured, Mary Grace, that we will work quietly to resolve this problem. Meanwhile, I hope you know that one bad person does not represent this school, which is full of smart and kind young people and adults who genuinely welcome you here."

"Thank you, Mrs. Stuart," said Grandma Cathy. "Please keep us posted on what you find out."

Mary Grace had a funny thought: *If this weren't about me, I'd think of it as an interesting mystery to solve!*

Mom said I would be safe and happy in California. Boy, was she wrong . . .

Although she was trying to appear brave, Mary Grace was scared. She was *not* safe, and she definitely was *not* happy. She thought about calling her mom, but something told her that she should handle this on her own. She suddenly felt very alone.

Mary Grace simply wanted to get all of this behind her, and she knew there was only one way to do that.

Mary Grace needed to solve the mystery.

Mary Grace started out by thinking long and hard about the notes: *Who wrote them? How did they get in my desk? When did they get put in my desk? Why were the notes sent to me?* She was stumped, but she had an idea.

That night, she asked Grandma Cathy if maybe the Grandma Gang could help her.

"I know *one* of us is happy to help," Grandma Cathy said. "And I bet the others will be too. I'll call La Shana and Elizabeth and invite them over for coffee and cookies tomorrow afternoon."

"Thanks, Grandma. You're the best."

At lunch the next day, Mary Grace told Ms. Root all about the Grandma Gang, and that they might help her solve the mystery.

"I think I read about them," her teacher said. "They are the ladies who solved the break-ins at the 7-Eleven, right? That was your grandmother?"

"Yep, that was her," Mary Grace said with pride.

"Well, I think you picked the right people to help you," said Ms. Root, happy that her new student was so resourceful.

"Ever since Grandma Cathy told me about the 7-Eleven case, I have wanted to work with you," said Mary Grace to her grandmother's friends. "But I never dreamed it would be to solve *my own* mystery!"

She proceeded to show the Grandma Gang copies of the two notes. Mrs. Stuart had kept the originals for her own official investigation.

Shocked at what they read, the ladies were appalled by the notes, and assured Mary Grace that they would do everything they could to help her. They were fully engaged and began throwing out questions, theories, and suggestions.

"Maybe someone saw who put the notes in your desk," said La Shana. "Do you think someone might come forward if they knew somebody from the sheriff's office was involved?" La Shana had been a sheriff herself and still worked part-time at the office. Her grandson Tyler was in fourth grade at North Elementary School. "I can call Mrs. Stuart and arrange to come to school and talk to each class about bullying."

"That's a great idea," said Mary Grace. "You should wear your old sheriff's uniform."

"You're right," said La Shana. "That will show that I mean business." She couldn't wait to put on her uniform again—and hoped she could still fit into it.

When La Shana spoke with Mrs. Stuart, the principal was so pleased by the thought of her visit that she offered to arrange a special assembly the very next Monday.

At eleven o'clock sharp, the students assembled in the gymnasium. They were told this was a serious event, but to them, it felt like an extension of recess. They milled around, chatting and laughing, until Mrs. Stuart stepped onto the stage with La Shana in her full uniform, including hat and badge.

The assembly was both instructive and very serious. La Shana explained that bullying came in many different forms and that it did not have to include pushing or shoving, or even a face-to-face encounter. It could even be something written on paper. She paused to let that sink in, and studied the students' faces for any extreme reactions. Mary Grace did the same.

"I'll be remaining at school for the rest of the day today," she said at the end of her talk. "So, if any of you have questions or you want to tell me about something you have seen or heard, I want you to come find me right away." The assembly talk was not long, but it was effective.

La Shana wandered the hallways for the next few hours, paying special attention to Room Twenty-Five. She saw nothing out of the ordinary, but she could sense that her presence was having an effect on the children. Although none of them came to her with any specific information, her message was received loud and clear by at least one student.

Two days later, Mary Grace found another sealed white envelope in her desk, addressed to her, once again, in purple Sharpie.

> I told you snitches get stitches and you brought in the sheriff.

> You're in big trouble now and so is your retard brother and your wimpy friend Penelope too.

> Watch out!

CHAPTER

THIRTEEN

Mary Grace waited at her desk for everyone to leave the classroom before showing the note to Ms. Root—who was stunned when she saw it.

"Mary Grace, I'm afraid this situation is getting worse," she said. "The first note was name-calling. The second note was threatening. And this third note is threatening harm to not only you and Donny, but also to poor Penelope as well."

"It's so unfair, Ms. Root," said Mary Grace. "Penelope didn't do anything! She doesn't even know about the notes. I haven't told anyone."

"I'm afraid we'll have to tell her now. Why don't you let me make a copy of this one for you to take home, and I'll give the original to Mrs. Stuart. Is your grandmother picking you and Donny up today?"

"Yes, ma'am."

"Why don't I walk you out to meet her? Just to be on the safe side."

Mrs. Stuart and Ms. Root sat in the principal's office, discussing the situation. The third note lay unfolded on Mrs. Stuart's desk.

"You did the right thing, Elaine, walking Mary Grace and Donny to their grandmother's car," Mrs. Stuart said to Ms. Root. "I simply can't bear the thought of anyone threatening our students—especially new and vulnerable ones."

"I know. I thought this kind of thing only happened in high school," replied Ms. Root.

"Children grow up so fast these days and get such strange ideas. I think I need to make a few calls. We live in very different times now."

First, Mrs. Stuart called someone on the school board to discuss what steps should be taken. She also called the school security officer to ask him to watch out for Donny, Mary Grace, and Penelope and make sure that no one bothered them. She then wrote a memo to all the teachers, before making more phone calls.

She called Grandma Cathy to tell her about the precautions she intended to take, wrote a memo to teachers advising them of the situation, and finally, she called Penelope's parents.

Penelope's mother was shocked that things like this still happen.

"I am used to the name-calling that I myself get sometimes," she said to Mrs. Stuart with a sigh, "but I just don't want my daughter to go through it. Thank you, Mrs. Stuart, for alerting me and for taking these steps to ensure the safety of your students." She agreed to pick up Penelope each day, at least until the school found the person writing the notes and saw that he or she was punished.

Mrs. Stuart also called Mrs. Hagen, who assured Mrs. Stuart that she would not let Donny out of her sight.

Mary Grace called Penelope that night, and when her friend answered, she said, "Pen, I feel so bad that you're involved in *my* mess."

"I feel so bad for *you*, Mary Grace," said Penelope. "Why didn't you tell me about all of this sooner? I mean . . . I wish you had told me. How long has it been going on?"

"A couple of weeks. I wanted to tell you, but I just—I guess I didn't want to make a big deal out of nothing. But the last note was scary."

"I wish I could help you, Mary Grace, but I don't know what to do! I feel so helpless. My friend is being bullied—and I can't help."

"Well, maybe you *can* help me, Pen."

"How?"

"You can help me solve this mystery."

"Oh, Mary Grace, I know you love mysteries and stuff, but this is *real*, not some story in a book! You could be in danger, and so could Donny. So could *I*."

"I know it's real, but if I don't work on solving it, I'll just go crazy. I know it's scary, but the only way I can handle it is to treat it like a mystery—a mystery that I have to solve. So I've been thinking about it, and I have an idea I want to talk to you about."

"Okay, I get it. If you treat it like a mystery, then it's not as scary."

"That's right. I am simply trying to solve this mystery. I am just trying to figure out who is writing these notes and putting them in my desk."

"What's the idea?"

"Well, last year, my fourth-grade teacher in Wichita, Mr. Claypool, put a shoebox on his desk. It was wrapped in colorful construction paper, and the top had a slit in it. He told us we should write him notes about anything that was on our minds—anything we wanted him to know about—and put our messages into the box through the slit. So, I was thinking . . . maybe there are kids who know something about the notes but are afraid to speak up. If we give them a way to leave a secret note about it, we might get some answers. What do you think?"

"Mary Grace, that is a great idea! It's definitely worth a try. Who knows? Maybe the person who wrote the notes in the first place feels bad about it now, and is ready to confess."

"I don't know about that, but let's talk to Ms. Root about it tomorrow. Meanwhile, I'm going to run it by the Grandma Gang."

"The what? What is the Grandma Gang?"

"Long story, Pen. I'll tell you all about it tomorrow."

"What a good idea!" said Grandma Cathy when Mary Grace told her about the shoebox. "Giving young people a way of speaking their minds safely is always a good thing."

"Do you think we should ask the rest of the Grandma Gang what they think?"

"I just got off the phone with Elizabeth. I told both her and La Shana about the third note, and they were quite upset about it. La Shana said that in situations like these, time is of the essence—meaning, she hopes we can solve it *fast* before things get worse. I think I can speak for the Grandma Gang when I say that your idea is a good one. They will love your shoebox idea."

Mary Grace had FaceTimed, texted, or emailed her parents every night since landing in California, but she still had not told them about the notes. That night, alone in her dark bedroom, she finally decided to share her troubles with them:

> I don't want you to freak out, but I thought I should tell you that I am having a problem at school.

> I am being bullied. Grandma and my teachers are great, but it's scary.

> I am scared.

> I miss you guys.

> I still want to go home.

Mary Grace read over what she wrote and was surprised by her own honesty. *They might as well know the truth,* she thought, *even if there's nothing they can do about it.* Her index finger hovered over the Send button, and a tear rolled down her cheek as she thought about her parents receiving this bad news. Then she pulled her finger away.

On second thought, what's the point of worrying them? Mary Grace decided that there was no reason to worry her parents, who would only feel as helpless as she did.

She nodded to herself and told herself that this was a problem she would have to solve on her own—and hit the Delete button.

Just after lunch on the day that Mary Grace and Penelope told Ms. Root about the shoebox idea, a beautifully decorated box appeared on the teacher's desk. She explained its purpose to the class and encouraged them to write notes about anything that might be bothering them around school or outside of it.

"Tell me anything you want," she said. "Tell me that you don't understand the homework. Tell me that you think I'm boring. Tell me that you think someone is cheating in class. Tell me that my blouse doesn't match my skirt. I promise you, I won't get mad, and I will take what you write seriously. Well . . . I might get a *little* mad if too many of you say I am boring!" She waited for the class to finish laughing and continued. "And I will keep everything you say in strict confidence if that is what you want. This is a safe and anonymous way to get important things off your mind and get a grown-up involved in anything you can't handle on your own. You know what *anonymous* means, right? It means nobody will know it's you!"

Ms. Root had done a great job of making the shoebox sound like a cool new idea that was good for everyone—but Mary Grace hoped it would be *bad* for the bully.

After recess the next morning, Ms. Root shook the box. There was definitely something in it, but she decided not to open it until lunchtime, when she would be alone in the classroom.

There were two notes in the shoebox. The first one read:

> The cafeteria has sour milk and stale cookies.

The second one read:

> Some things are going on in this class but I'm not ready to talk about them.

When the kids came back from lunch, Ms. Root began their social studies lesson without making any mention of the notes.

The next day during lunchtime, Ms. Root checked the box again. This time, there was just one note:

Tiffany Johnson spends every lunchtime crying in the girl's bathroom but she won't tell anyone why she's crying.

Hmmm, thought Ms. Root, *Tiffany is a friend of Mary Grace and Penelope. I wonder if she is being bullied too?* She stopped Tiffany on her way into class after lunch and quietly asked her to stay for a few minutes after school.

When the final bell rang and all the other kids rushed out of the classroom, Tiffany stayed behind, stacking and restacking her books. When everyone was finally gone, she walked up to Ms. Root's desk, her eyes focused on her shoes. When she looked up, the teacher could see that she'd been crying—and might start again at any moment.

"Tiffany, can you tell me what's the matter?" Ms. Root said gently.

"Oh, Ms. Root . . . I did something awful and I don't know what to do about it."

Ms. Root waited quietly for Tiffany to say more.

"I . . . I cheated on my last math test! I wrote some of the formulas on a tissue. I figured, if anyone saw me, I could just use the tissue and blow my nose and . . . hide the evidence!"

Cheating was a serious thing, of course, but Ms. Root was a bit relieved that this was all that had been bothering Tiffany. It was certainly better than being threatened.

"Tiffany, that makes me unhappy, but I'm glad you told me about it. We will discuss the consequences of cheating, but let's also talk about getting you some extra help in math so you won't feel the *need* to cheat—okay?"

But Tiffany didn't look relieved. Her face got even redder.

"It's much worse than that," she said, her voice getting a little trembly.

"How so?" Ms. Root asked.

"After the test, Justin Green came up to me and said he saw me cheating. He said he was going to tell you about it—unless I did something for him."

"My goodness! What did he want you to do?"

"He said I had to put these notes in Mary Grace's desk."

Bingo.

"Go on," Ms. Root said, knowing that Mary Grace's box idea seemed to have worked as planned.

"Justin gave me the first note without an envelope, and I read it. It was so mean! I knew I shouldn't put it in Mary Grace's desk because it would hurt her feelings, but I did it anyway. I don't know if it was because I was scared of Justin or scared of *you*. There were two more notes after that, but they were both in envelopes, so I couldn't read them. I figured they were just as mean as the first one, but by then,

I . . . oh, Ms. Root, I feel so bad about it. I haven't been able to sleep or eat or study or anything!"

"Thank you very much for sharing this with me, Tiffany. It's never too late to do the right thing. Tell me, did Justin say why he wrote these notes?"

"He said he thinks Mary Grace is a stuck-up loser and that her brother is a weirdo who always has a big, goofy smile on his face. He said they don't belong in our school, and he's going to make sure they hate it so much, they leave. The thing is . . . I sort of want them to leave too. Before Mary Grace came here, Penelope was *my* best friend. Now she spends all her time with Mary Grace, and I feel left out. So maybe that's partly why I went along with it."

"You should know, Tiffany, that Mrs. Stuart and I are aware of the notes. Mary Grace shared them with us because they frightened her so badly."

Tiffany looked down at her feet.

"I would never want Mary Grace to be scared—not really. And I especially wouldn't want to upset Donny. He's a sweet kid, and it's so cool the way she looks out for him. I guess I just . . . wasn't thinking straight. I wanted Penelope all to myself. I know how stupid that must sound." After saying it out loud, Tiffany realized that it didn't just *sound* stupid; it *was* stupid.

"Oh, Tiffany, you certainly made a mistake. We all make them. You still have a lot to learn about friends and friendships. But . . . what's important is what we do about our mistakes."

"I don't know *what* to do about it, Ms. Root. I swear, I was going to write you a note all about it and put it in the box, but . . . I knew that wouldn't make it right."

"Tiffany, sometimes even teachers don't know exactly what to do right away, so let's think it over. But first . . ." She stepped forward and hugged Tiffany tight.

Tiffany needed that hug desperately, and sagged a little in Ms. Root's arms.

"We will get through this, Tiffany, mainly by continuing to be honest." She reached into her desk drawer and pulled out a wad of tissues, which she handed to Tiffany.

Ms. Root suddenly realized that hugging a student may be against some rule—but this girl had needed a hug. *Oh well. I will simply apologize for caring too much if I am brought in front of the school board.*

"The first thing you must realize is that Justin's threat is meaningless now. You have told the truth about cheating, so he has no power over you. Second, I want you to know that both Mary Grace and Penelope were threatened in those notes, and they are both very worried about it."

"Penelope too? That's terrible!"

"I am going to speak with Mrs. Stuart, and she or I will call your mother to set up a conference—probably tomorrow after school. I suggest you tell your mother the whole story before we meet. And please keep in mind that no students but Mary Grace and Penelope know about the notes, and that is the way they'd like to keep it for now. Please don't talk to anyone else at school about the matter. If you need to talk, come to me or call me on my cell phone." She quickly scribbled her number on an index card and handed it to Tiffany.

"My mom is going to freak. I'm in *big* trouble," said Tiffany. "But I guess I feel . . . better. It was a hard secret to keep."

As Ms. Root left her classroom, she saw Mrs. Hagen coming down the hall.

"Cheryl, do you have a minute?" Ms. Root asked, and gave her a quick rundown of all that Tiffany had told her. "I'm on my way to tell Bertha about it now," she said as they parted. "Honestly, I cannot wait to have a few words with that Justin and his parents!"

"Sorry to bother you so late on a Thursday afternoon, but I have some big news," Ms. Root said to Mrs. Stuart before sharing the details with her.

The principal replied, "Well, it looks like I have a few decisions to make—and a lot of calls."

"Let me know if I can help, Bertha," said Ms. Root. It's a sticky situation, I know, and I think the girls trust me to be on their side."

"Thank you, Elaine. I think the first step is to gather all of the information we can before we deal with Justin."

FOURTEEN

"Mrs. Stuart called after school today," Grandma Cathy announced to her granddaughter.

"You were on the phone for a *long* time! I was wondering who you were talking to."

"They found out who wrote those terrible notes and who put them in your desk."

"They *did!?* Who was it?"

"Well actually, it was *two* people, sweetheart. One of them wrote the notes, and another put them in your desk."

"Who? Who are they?" Mary Grace was anxious to hear the names.

"Justin Green and Tiffany Johnson."

"Tiffany!? But she's my friend. Well, sort of. And she's not even friends with Justin."

After Grandma Cathy explained exactly what had happened, Mary Grace thought for a few seconds, then said, "What's going to happen to them?"

"I'm not exactly sure, honey, but I know that Mrs. Stuart and your teachers are going to handle it so that these children learn that bullying is a serious matter, and that the school needs to report it and do what the law requires."

"What does the law require?"

"California state law requires that each school district have a formal policy to help identify and punish bullying behavior. I don't know exactly what this school district's policy is—but all the policies are very strict." Grandma Cathy sounded like the lawyer that she was.

"Do you know what the punishments are?"

"No. Not yet. Mrs. Stuart just found out. Ms. Root talked to Tiffany less than an hour ago. They still need to gather all the facts. Nobody has even talked to Justin yet."

"How did Ms. Root find out it was Justin and Tiffany?" asked Mary Grace, trying to piece things together in her mind. *Why hadn't she figured it out herself?*

"Well, that is thanks to your great idea, Mary Grace," said Grandma Cathy. "It all started with a note somebody left in the box on Ms. Root's desk."

"That is *soooo* cool!" said Mary Grace, thrilled that the shoebox was involved.

"Your idea helped solve the mystery."

"We've got to tell the Grandma Gang! I want them to know that I would make a great member—even if I'm not a grandma!"

"Well, today is Thursday, our day to play bridge at Gigi's. Why don't you grab Donny from his room and bring him over there with me."

"Sure thing, Grandma. And I'll make sure he brings his marbles."

The three of them were the first to arrive at Gigi's condo. Grandma Cathy had called ahead, so Gigi had already put out milk and cookies for the kids. She fawned over Mary Grace and Donny, as usual, until La Shana and Elizabeth arrived a short time later.

"Donny, Ed should be here with his mother any minute now," said Gigi. "He can't wait to see you again, and I think he's hoping you'll go back to his place to play."

"Yesss," said Donny. "I brought some *new* marbles this time. Maybe Ed will want to trade with me." Donny held out both his hands, with six or so marbles in each.

"Boy, those are some nice-looking marbles, Donny," said Elizabeth. "Are you sure you want to trade them away?"

"Maybe Ed has even better ones!"

There was a knock at the door, and before Gigi could get to it, Donny was racing for the front hall, shouting, ""That must be Ed!" When he pulled the door open—sure enough—Ed was standing there beaming beside his mom.

"Hi, Ed," said Donny, "let's go to your house!" Donny started walking as if he knew where he was going.

"It's this way, Donny!" Ed called out.

"Oops!" said Donny, laughing and running back toward Ed. "Bye, Grandma!" he shouted, and the two walked off in the right direction, like best friends.

"Thank you, Mrs. Knight, for hosting Donny," said Grandma Cathy.

"Thank *you*. It is so nice for Ed to have someone to play with," she replied, following after her son and his new friend.

When Donny and the Knights were gone, Mary Grace and the Grandma Gang sat down around the kitchen table, where the cards and notepads had been laid out for bridge.

"Ladies," said Grandma Cathy, "before we play cards, Mary Grace has something she wants to tell you all."

The chitchat stopped, and all eyes turned to Mary Grace.

"What is it, dear?" asked Elizabeth.

"Well . . . I knew you'd be interested in the solution to the puzzle of the mysterious notes." She paused dramatically. "Grandma and I got some news from school today about who wrote them and who put them in my desk. I just couldn't wait to share it," she said before once again pausing dramatically and looking around the table at everybody.

"Good gracious!" said La Shana. "Do tell!"

"It was actually *two* people!" said Mary Grace.

"Who?" asked La Shana.

"How'd they find out who did it?" asked Elizabeth.

"Did they catch them red-handed?" asked Gigi. "We need details! Who, what, when, where, how?"

Mary Grace could not keep track of who was asking the questions. These women were as excited as she was that the mystery had been solved.

"Mary Grace," said Grandma Cathy, "is it okay if I explain how those scoundrels were tracked down? It would give me a chance to brag about my granddaughter, and you know I love doing that." Grandma Cathy was beaming.

"No way, Grandma. I want to be the one to tell them about the shoebox." She put both hands over her mouth when she realized she'd given away the best part.

"Your idea for the special box worked!" said La Shana, leaning forward to give Mary Grace a high five while the others clapped their hands.

"Gigi's namesake is a smart cookie," said Grandma Cathy proudly.

"With the help of the Grandma Gang," Mary Grace said as she waved her hand around the table at the women.

After sharing the rest of the details, Mary Grace confessed that she was a bit worried about what the other kids at school would say when the news got out.

"I'm afraid that somehow Justin and Tiffany might turn the story around and make Penelope and me look like losers," she said.

"That is not very likely," said Elizabeth. "Those two won't want the story going around any more than you do."

The others nodded in agreement.

"I just want people to leave me and Donny alone," said Mary Grace, "and treat us like everybody else. Especially Donny."

"Is there anything we can do to help?" La Shana asked. "Since you are an official member of the Grandma Gang now?"

"Well, I was thinking . . ." said Mary Grace. She paused for a second, then looked right at La Shana. "I know that Justin and Tiffany will be punished at school, and probably at home too. That's what they are expecting—but maybe you could get somebody from the sheriff's office to explain that it could have been much worse. If they break the law when they're older, whether it's harassment or something else, like stealing, they could get arrested! And go to jail! Not just get punished by their principal."

"Hmm," said La Shana. "Let me talk to Deputy Juan. I bet he'd be willing to arrange a visit to your school to tell these two exactly how serious this kind of behavior really is."

"That would be great," said Mary Grace. Thank you. It's pretty special to have the Grandma Gang on my side!"

"You bet we're on your side," said Elizabeth. "Now let's teach you some bridge!"

Mary Grace was happy to know that she had the Grandma Gang on her side.

"You know what's kind of weird?" Mary Grace mused as the ladies reached for the cards. "Justin doesn't even know he is in trouble yet."

The next day, Tiffany's mother was scheduled to come in to Mrs. Stuart's office to meet with her and the teachers. Tiffany was required to attend as well, of course, and she'd tossed and turned half the night, worrying about it.

Mrs. Hagen was the first to arrive, followed by Ms. Root, who quickly recapped for the other two what Tiffany had told her. She passed out copies of the three notes to each of them to be sure they were aware of every word they contained.

Mrs. Stuart then shared some information she felt the teachers should have: "While Tiffany has no disciplinary record at our school," she said, "Justin is a different matter. He has been in one kind of trouble or another ever since his grandmother died about a year ago. His grandmother had been taking care of him while his dad worked two jobs to make the money they needed. Now that she's gone, I'm afraid he's run a bit wild. I honestly wish I'd been more actively involved in the matter, but—well . . . we have so many students, and—"

There was a light knock at Mrs. Stuart's door, and then Tiffany's mother walked in, followed by Tiffany. The looks on their faces told the others that there had already been a lot of discussion between them about the seriousness of what Tiffany did.

"Why don't you both take seats and we'll get started," said Mrs. Stuart. Mrs. Johnson, I'm not sure you have met Mrs. Hagen, our special education teacher."

Once the necessary greetings had been exchanged and copies of the notes passed to Mrs. Johnson, Ms. Root said, "I am not sure how much Tiffany has told you about what happened to necessitate this meeting, but she has confessed to being the one who left these notes in Mary Grace's desk. It was admirable for her to come forward. We are also aware that Tiffany did not write these notes, but was asked to deliver them by another student—Justin Green."

Tiffany had, in fact, told her mother everything the night before, but she had seen only the first note. Mrs. Johnson quickly read the notes, then passed them to her daughter, who read them also.

Tiffany's lower lip trembled as she placed the papers in her lap, and after a few seconds, tears leaked from her eyes. "I-I-I ... didn't know how ... awful they were," she said, sniffling and reaching across Mrs. Stuart's desk for a tissue from the box that always sat there. "I feel so guilty for hurting Mary Grace and Penelope! I'd be so scared if somebody left a note in my desk that read, 'Snitches get stitches'!" She blew her nose into the tissue and sank back into her chair, looking miserable.

"Good heavens, Tiffany," said Mrs. Johnson, "I can't believe you were involved in this! These girls are your friends!"

"Mom, I'm *soooo* sorry," Tiffany said between sniffles.

"Mrs. Stuart," said Mrs. Johnson, "I want you to know that Tiffany will do whatever you think is best to help make this right—and she will accept whatever punishment you feel she deserves. Isn't that right, Tiffany?"

"Y-y-yes," she whimpered.

"Thank you—both of you—for being so cooperative today," said Mrs. Stuart, "but this is a delicate situation. These teachers and I need a bit more time to figure out the best course of action. We'll be asking you to come back and meet with us again, probably on Monday morning. Meanwhile, for the sake of everyone involved, we'd ask that you not discuss this with anyone. Tiffany, do you understand me? I do not want you talking about this with any of your friends at school—is that clear?"

"Yes, Mrs. Stuart," Tiffany said, punctuating her statement with one more honk into the tissue.

"We understand, Mrs. Stuart. Thank you for your time," said Mrs. Johnson, standing and smoothing her skirt.

"Tiffany," said Ms. Root, "in the meantime, I suggest you start thinking about how you might make amends with your friends. They have every reason to be quite angry with you right now."

"Yes, ma'am."

"I think that went well," said Mrs. Stuart to the teachers after the Johnsons had left her office. "I think we should deal with Tiffany on Monday and Justin on Tuesday."

"Of course," said Ms. Root. "Please feel free to call me over the weekend to talk about it."

"I am sure I will. I will probably need to ask you for more information . . . and I will probably need to ask for your advice," said Mrs. Stuart with a shrug. "This is a tricky situation, at best, and it is going to be a busy weekend."

FIFTEEN

On Monday, Mrs. Stuart met with Tiffany and Mrs. Johnson in the principal's conference room, in the presence of Ms. Root, La Shana, and Deputy Juan.

Mrs. Stuart started out by repeating her appreciation for Tiffany's honesty and cooperation.

"But," she added, "Tiffany, I have thought about this a lot, and I feel I have no choice but to suspend you for a day."

Tiffany didn't say anything—just looked down at her hands folded in her lap.

"This is the minimum punishment I can require, based on the school's zero-tolerance policy on bullying."

"We understand, Mrs. Stuart," said Mrs. Johnson. "And I think that is fair. I want you to know that Tiffany is also being punished at home. She has been grounded for a month, and won't be able to see her friends or participate in any activities outside of school. And—what's worse, according to Tiffany—her dad and I have taken away her cell phone for a month."

Everyone but Tiffany chuckled a little at this. Then Tiffany handed Mrs. Stuart three envelopes, each one addressed to a different person.

"I wrote notes to Penelope and Mary Grace, telling them how sorry I am. I promised never to hurt or be mean to them ever again."

"That was a nice thing to do, Tiffany," said Mrs. Stuart, "but what is in the third envelope I'm holding?"

"I . . . also wrote a note to you and Ms. Root. I wanted to explain why I did what I did, and all about how Justin threatened me."

"I see. Thank you, Tiffany. We will read and consider what you wrote."

"There's one more thing, Mrs. Stuart," said Tiffany. "My mom and I discussed how actions speak louder than words. So I thought of a way to show my friends how sorry I am—especially for anything bad that might have happened to Donny. I would like to volunteer in Donny's classroom for the next three months. I could go in after school and help Mrs. Hagen clean up and prepare for the next day."

"Well, now you are really thinking, Tiffany," said Mrs. Stuart. "I am very nicely surprised at your generosity and remorse, and I'm sure Mrs. Hagen will be happy for the help. In fact, I have to say that until now, I have never had a student punish *herself* more severely than the school has punished her."

Everyone laughed at this, and the meeting ended on a high note.

On Tuesday morning, Mrs. Stuart called Justin's father and asked if she could meet with him after school.

"Today?!" barked Mr. Green. "That won't be easy. I can't get there by three. Even if I can get off early, I can't be there before four. I'll have to talk to my boss and get back to you."

Mrs. Stuart could hear loud banging noises in the background as Mr. Green spoke.

"I know you are very busy, Mr. Green. This is important, or I would not be bothering you at work. We can be flexible here— just let me know when you are coming. We'll keep Justin at school until you get here."

"Did he do something wrong?"

"I think it's best if we discuss everything in person."

After she hung up, Mrs. Stuart thought about the fact that Mr. Green had not asked if Justin was okay. She shrugged and sent a text message to Ms. Root, saying that the meeting with Mr. Green was on, and that she should speak with Justin before the meeting. "He may be more open talking with you one-on-one," she wrote, "and without his father around."

Ms. Root asked Justin to meet with her at lunchtime, so when his classmates left for the cafeteria, Justin walked up and stood in front of Ms. Root's desk, looking at his feet.

"Justin," she began, "I wonder if you know why I've asked you to speak with me?"

"Um . . . I guess," he replied, still not looking at her. "Is it about . . . the notes?"

"Yes, Justin. It's about the notes. Tiffany has filled us in on what happened, and has expressed how sorry she is for her part in it. But now I'd like to hear what you have to say. Can you tell me what you said to Tiffany—and what you wrote in that note—about Mary Grace's brother, Donny?"

"I might have said that he's a retard," Justin said, still looking down at his feet.

"Anything else?"

"I might have also said that he and Mary Grace should move back to where they came from."

"Do you think that word is appropriate?" Ms. Root asked.

"Um . . . people use that word. And I'm not the only one who calls the Classroom Five kids 'retards.' Even my dad uses that word, about a guy at work who's really dumb. I guess I thought it was funny."

"Well, I'm afraid *I* don't find it funny, and neither did Mary Grace. She was very upset, and with good reason. Why on earth would you have written such terrible things to her—a new student who just wants to feel welcome here?"

"I may have written those notes, but Tiffany is the one who put them in Mary Grace's desk!" Justin shouted. "She's the one who should get in trouble, not me!"

"Oh, Justin, I think the time has come for you to be honest. Tiffany was very troubled by what she did, and she has told us everything—all about your threats and what you made her do. And she has done more than that, Justin. She has apologized and figured out a way to make up for her part in this."

Justin stood silently, shifting his weight from one foot to the other.

"But we are not here to talk about Tiffany. Let's talk about you. From what I understand, you threatened Tiffany in order to make her put your very unkind notes in Mary Grace's desk. And in those notes, you insulted Mary Grace and her brother and threatened to hurt them, along with another classmate, Penelope. Does that sum it up?"

"I . . . guess . . . but Tiffany cheated on her math test! I saw her!"

"Yes, Justin, I am aware of that. And fear of exposure is what motivated her to help you. But . . . that doesn't solve the problem you and I have right now. That doesn't make what you did right—does it?"

Justin said nothing.

"Oh, Justin. I know you've been really sad about losing your grandmother. It must be so difficult for you and your father. I remember losing my grandmother; I was sad for a long time. But sadness is not an excuse to be mean to those around you. I believe you need to think a lot harder about what you did and how it made your classmates feel. I think when you have really thought about it, you'll know what you have to do. But let's start with a promise that you will never do such things again. You will never bully or threaten or call someone a name again. Can you at least promise me that? And, if you ever feel sad and want to talk to somebody about it, I'm here to listen."

"I . . . I guess so," Justin replied, looking at the ground and wishing he could be anywhere else but in that room.

"I want you to know that you'll be staying after school today. Mrs. Stuart has called your father, and he is leaving work early to come here for a meeting. After the last bell, I want you to go to Mrs. Stuart's office and wait for him."

"He's coming here?"

"Yes, he is. And I imagine he is not happy about it."

For a second, Justin looked genuinely afraid—but then his expression changed to a sneer.

"Can I go now?" he asked.

"Yes, Justin, you may."

As he turned leave, Ms. Root heard him mutter, "Tiffany, Mary Grace, and Penelope are all tattletales. They'll be sorry."

"Justin Green, please come back here."

He turned, but stayed rooted to his spot halfway between Ms. Root's desk and the door.

"We are not done here, young man. Do you understand that you just threatened your classmates *again?* After promising me you wouldn't?"

"But they—"

"This isn't about *them*, Justin; it is about *you* and your actions. You are not going to make anyone 'sorry.' The only one who should be very, very sorry right now is you."

His "Yes, ma'am," was so quiet, Ms. Root could barely hear it.

"Justin, how can I make you understand that words and actions have consequences? Yours have gotten you in deep, deep trouble. If I had to guess, I'd think Mrs. Stuart is deciding whether to suspend you or expel you altogether."

"I could be expelled?!"

"Yes, Justin, depending on how you handle yourself, starting right this minute, you could be expelled from North Elementary School. What you did is bullying, and we cannot stand for that."

Justin was silent for a moment, then said, "My father is going to freak out."

"For now, I suggest you keep all of this to yourself and be on your best behavior. We all make mistakes, Justin, but how we deal with them is what matters more than anything. You can't change what you did, but you can learn from it and try to make up for it. That is something to think about between now and the end of the day."

For the first time since the bell rang, Justin looked directly at Ms. Root, which moved her to take a kinder tone.

"Justin, would you prefer to wait with me after school, here in my classroom instead of in the principal's office? We can walk down there together if you'd like."

"Um, yeah, maybe I will. I think my dad is going to be pretty mad."

"All right, then. Just stay after the last bell, and you and I can discuss how to make your dad a little less mad."

Without another word, Justin walked out of the room and headed for the cafeteria.

Mr. Green showed up just after four o'clock. As he entered the principal's conference room, he saw Justin surrounded by Mrs. Stuart, Ms. Root, Mrs. Hagen, and—to his great surprise—two people in sheriff's uniforms. That's when he understood how serious the meeting really was. La Shana and Deputy Juan were standing off to the side, observing the proceedings.

"What have you done this time?" Mr. Green demanded of his son.

"I don't know, Dad. I swear, I don't even know why we're here."

"I think you do, Justin," said Ms. Root. "Remember our talk, especially the part about admitting our mistakes?"

Mrs. Stuart quickly filled in Mr. Green on what Justin had done. As he listened, he kept looking over at his son, who was sinking down lower and lower in his seat.

"I must tell you, Mr. Green," Mrs. Stuart said firmly, "our school takes a very dim view of such behavior. In fact, we have a zero-tolerance policy for bullying. We are here to discuss whether Justin should be suspended or expelled from North Elementary School."

Mr. Green wrinkled his forehead at Mrs. Stuart—the words *bullying, suspended,* and *expelled* had come through loud and clear.

"Three notes were written and put inside the desk of a young girl who is new in the class," Mrs. Stuart stated, "and Justin has admitted that he wrote all three notes."

"I would like you to read these notes, Mr. Green."

Mrs. Stuart dramatically placed the first note in front of him.

Mr. Green read the notes quickly and shook his head.

"Yeah, Dad. They want to suspend me for using the word *retard.* Can you believe it?"

"You're the retard, Justin," Mr. Green said, turning to his son. "Why do you do such hurtful things?"

"Mr. Green!" exclaimed Mrs. Stuart, "we don't tolerate that kind of language in our school. And we don't approve of adults calling our students names, even if the adult in question is the child's own father."

"I—I'm sorry, ma'am, but . . . I swear, I don't know where this kid gets his crazy ideas from."

"Let's move on. Since Justin decided to target a young boy in our special education class, I've asked his teacher to explain just how hurtful and—dare I say *ignorant*—that truly is."

Directing her words to both Mr. Green and Justin, Mrs. Hagen patiently explained some facts about Down syndrome.

Afterward, she said, "While it is true that Donny needs to be in a special class, and that he may never be able to do some of the things that Justin and his friends can do, he is a wonderful and very interesting little boy with many skills. Donny is kind, optimistic, and enthusiastic. He has an amazing memory and loves to learn. He is very kind to others, and he especially loves his big sister, Mary Grace. I want you both to understand that Donny and Mary Grace are treasured additions to our school community and deserve to be treated as they treat others: with kindness and respect."

"Thank you, Mrs. Hagen," said Mrs. Stuart. "I couldn't agree more."

Mr. Green pushed his chair out and started to get up.

"Okay, okay," he said. "You made your point. I'm not the father of the year, and Justin screwed up. Thanks for pointing it out. I'll take care of it at home. You don't need to worry about it." He glared at Justin, who sank even lower in his chair.

"I'm sorry, Mr. Green, but that is not how it works," said Mrs. Stuart forcefully. "I appreciate the fact that Justin is your son, but we have rules and responsibilities too. Especially in light of the fact that Justin actually threatened his fellow students in those notes."

"Aw, he didn't mean anything by that," said Mr. Green, sitting back down. "He was just being a wise guy."

"I don't agree, sir. 'Snitches get stitches'? That is a threat if ever there was one. That is why we have two members of law enforcement present. Perhaps neither you nor Justin realizes it, but making threats is punishable by law. In addition to writing the notes, Justin verbally threatened the girls. Ms. Root heard him do so; isn't that right, Ms. Root?"

"I'm afraid so," said Ms. Root. "Just this afternoon, standing in my classroom, he called Tiffany and her friends tattletales and said they'd 'be sorry.'"

"You can see now why we've asked deputies Juan and La Shana to be here," said Mrs. Stuart.

At the sound of their names, the two officials stepped forward.

"I don't know what action the sheriff's office will take," Deputy Juan said to Justin and his father, "but we will *not* take additional punitive action if we think the school has acted to identify the bullying, acted to stop the bullying, and acted to punish the offender to prevent future incidents. Threatening harm is another matter . . ."

Deputy Juan explained that threatening anyone with bodily harm is a crime. "Justin could be in big trouble, sir—and Tiffany, as well, for 'aiding and abetting' him. But . . . considering their age, we might decide to let the school and the families take the lead on punishment."

Something about the presence of the deputies got under Mr. Green's skin.

"What about free speech?" he asked, leaning forward. "Don't grade school kids have First Amendment rights, like everybody else?"

"Sorry, Mr. Green, but that does *not* apply to threats," La Shana said, quickly shutting him down. "In fact, the Supreme Court has ruled that threats of violence are not protected by the First Amendment. The Supreme Court decided that protecting individuals from the fear of violence, and the possibility that the threatened violence will occur, is more important than freedom of speech."

"So, as you just heard, threats *are* against the law," Mrs. Stuart emphasized, "and Justin will most likely *not* be charged. However, according to school district policy on bullying, Justin must be suspended and/or expelled for bullying another student—or *students,* as in this case."

She let that sink in before continuing: "Beginning tomorrow, Justin will be officially suspended for three days. We feel this is a fair and quite lenient punishment. And Justin, listen carefully to what I am about to say. Expulsion is still an option if I hear one whisper of any further misbehavior on your part. Do you understand me?"

"Yes, ma'am," said Justin, who was visibly shaken. Seeing those sheriffs had scared him. And when the other kids found out he was suspended, he'd be in for a lot of teasing. He certainly didn't want to be expelled and sent to another school.

Mrs. Stuart told Justin he would need to make up any work he missed and that he could not be on the school grounds or have contacts of any kind, including phone calls, texts, and emails, with any students until the following Monday. Then she took on a softer tone.

"Justin," the principal continued, "we know this all seems very harsh, but please understand that Ms. Root and I are on your side. We are not here to judge and embarrass you. In fact, we hope you will learn from this situation, straighten yourself out, and become the good and kind member of our community we know you can be. While you are away from school—and that means you cannot be anywhere near school grounds—you will be responsible for completing all homework assignments. The details of this meeting and what led up to it will be kept confidential by all concerned. While you're gone, I'd like you to think about how you'd like to apologize to those hurt by your conduct. It is my hope that you, Tiffany, and the students you wronged will all be able to put this behind you very soon. Does anyone have any questions?"

There was a minute of awkward silence before Mrs. Stuart dismissed the meeting.

CHAPTER

SIXTEEN

Mary Grace asked Grandma Cathy if she could talk with the Grandma Gang again.

"Sure, honey," said Grandma Cathy. "We are playing bridge on Thursday at Gigi's, as usual."

"Do you think we could invite Penelope and Mrs. Li?"

"That's a great idea. Poor Penelope was caught up in the little mess at school, and it would be nice to meet her mother. Why don't you invite them, and I'll tell Gigi to bake an extra batch of cookies—and figure on less time to play bridge."

Everyone showed up at Gigi's condo around four o'clock on Thursday and gathered around her big dining-room table.

She'd put out her famous butter cookies, tea for the adults, and milk for the kids. Mrs. Li had brought some special Chinese almond cookies and honeycomb cookies, and they were a big hit with everybody.

"I still like Snickerdoodles the best," Donny announced, but that didn't stop him from putting a third honeycomb cookie in his mouth, making everybody smile.

"Hey, Penelope, want to see my marbles?" Donny asked. He slapped a handful of them on the table, and they immediately started rolling every which way.

"Wow, Donny, those are pretty!" said Penelope, helping him gather them up before they fell to the floor. "Look, Mom, aren't Donny's marbles amazing?"

"Very nice, Donny," said Mrs. Li, "and that reminds me—I brought you something."

"Really? What?" Donny was very excited.

Mrs. Li reached into her handbag.

"I love surprises!" Donny hopped from one foot to the other as he waited anxiously for Mrs. Li to reveal what was in her purse.

"Good. Because I have *two* of them for you."

"Two surprises! *Two* surprises!" Donny announced, as everyone waited to see what Mrs. Li would pull out of her purse.

"First, I have a piece of paper for you."

"Paper!?"

Mrs. Li presented Donny with a beautiful paper lotus flower, elaborately folded in a special way that must have taken hours, even for someone with great skill.

"It's a flower!" Donny said "Not paper, silly."

"It is a flower that is made out of paper," Mrs. Li replied as Donny turned it over and over in his hands.

"Mrs. Li made it herself," said Mary Grace. "Isn't that incredible? It is like a little piece of art, so be careful with it, okay?"

Donny gently handed it to Grandma Cathy, who passed it around the table. Everybody *oohed* and *aahed* when it was their turn to hold it.

"What is the second surprise?" asked Donny.

"Well, I know you're going to like this one," said Mrs. Li, "because it is a marble—a special, good-luck one." Mrs. Li presented the marble to Donny.

"It has a number inside," Donny said, examining it closely.

"What number is it?" asked Mary Grace.

"One, two, three, four, five, six, seven…" Donny counted on his fingers. "It's eight!" he declared. "Eight?" Donny saw Mary Grace's eyes light up but he didn't know why. "It's eight! The number eight is inside the marble. Wait … why do we care about eight?"

Do you know why it is a lucky marble, Donny?" Mrs. Li asked.

"Why?"

"Because in China—where I come from—the number eight means good luck. I hope this marble brings you lots of good luck, Donny."

"Wow! That is so cool!"

"Say thank you to Mrs. Li, Donny," Grandma Cathy prompted.

Donny did more than say thank you. He got up from the table and gave Mrs. Li a big hug.

"Thank you for my lucky marble," he said, beaming. "I will *not* trade it to Ed, I promise."

"Thank Mrs. Li for the beautiful paper lotus flower too," Grandma Cathy added, and Donny hugged Mrs. Li again.

"Why, Donny," said Mrs. Li, nearly in tears, "you are the best person to give gifts to . . . because you give the best hugs in return!"

Just as Donny was going back to his seat near the cookies, there was a knock at the door.

"Ed's here! Bye!" Donny shouted as he ran off to answer the door. The second he opened it, he said, "Look, Ed, I have a lucky marble! Let's go."

"Bye, Donny," everyone shouted, but he and Ed were already halfway to Ed's condo for their playdate.

"What a sweet boy," said Mrs. Li, and everybody nodded in agreement.

"So, Mary Grace," said La Shana, while Gigi cleared the plates and got out the cards and pads, "why did you want to meet with us?"

"Yes," added Elizabeth, "we thought you'd already solved your mystery with the help of your shoebox idea."

"Yeah, what do you need *us* for? You seem to be doing fine on your own!" La Shana added.

"We did solve it," said Mary Grace, "but we need your opinions and ideas about something. I told Penelope how smart you all are, and how fun you are too. I guess I just wanted Penelope to meet you since I'm kind of in the Grandma Gang myself now!"

"Those are nice compliments, Mary Grace," said Elizabeth. "Thank you. We think you are smart and fun too. But, Penelope, get ready to see some old ladies who still think and act like they are twelve years old!"

When everybody had finished laughing over that, Mary Grace got to the point: "Okay, so here's what's happened since I saw you last," she began. "The school suspended Tiffany for one day and Justin for three days. Tiffany felt so bad about what she did that she wrote apology notes to me and Penelope, and she wants to work with Mrs. Hagen in Donny's classroom every day—so Pen and I think we can probably be friends with her again." She paused. "What we're worried about is Justin."

"Oh," said Grandma Cathy. "I guess I hadn't realized he was still a problem."

"Wait . . . Tiffany got suspended too? Why?" Elizabeth asked.

"Something about a 'zero-tolerance policy,'" Mary Grace said with a shrug.

Grandma Cathy explained that a zero-tolerance policy means that school officials are required to hand down specific, consistent, and harsh punishment—usually suspension or expulsion—when students break certain rules. The punishment applies regardless of the circumstances.

"Basically, Tiffany was involved in a bullying incident, so she must be suspended. Those are the rules. No exceptions," Grandma Cathy said.

"So Tiffany is back and has been nice to us, and Justin hasn't been in school, so things are good now," Penelope said, "but we are worried about when he gets back."

"Penelope and I . . . we just want the whole thing to just go away," said Mary Grace. "We just want everything to be kept secret from the other kids in school so they don't talk about us or call us 'snitches' or anything like that. Mrs. Stuart told Grandma that the school is talking about transferring Justin to the other fifth-grade class and giving him some kind of job around the school, like cleaning classrooms."

"Well, at least they seem to be taking what he did seriously," said Elizabeth, "and trying to teach him a lesson."

"Yeah," said Mary Grace, "but what about us? If Justin switches classrooms and all that stuff, kids will definitely wonder why—and they'll probably find out. And then they'll talk about us, and the whole thing will never be over!"

"Hmm . . . you're right. Kids will figure it out, and it will bring attention to you and Penelope and Donny," said La Shana, who understood their concern.

"So you want us to help you to figure out how to keep it all quiet until it blows over," said Elizabeth. "Is that right?"

"Yes!" said Mary Grace. "We have been thinking a lot about it, and it all comes down to one question: What is the best punishment for Justin that will actually be a good thing for *us?*"

"Before we even start this discussion," said Grandma Cathy, "I think there are some things that you all should know—things that even Mary Grace wasn't aware of until I told her yesterday."

All eyes turned to Grandma Cathy, who took a deep breath and continued: "Justin Green is an only child, and his mom has never been around. Luckily for him and his dad, his grandmother lived with them and helped take care of Justin all his life—until just a year ago. That's when Justin's grandmother died, and that made things very hard for him. Justin's dad is a decent, hardworking man who is doing the best he can, but, well . . . he just isn't around enough, and when he is, he's pretty tired from working two jobs. Justin has to spend a lot of time on his own. He probably misses his grandma and isn't getting enough love and guidance at home."

"Wow, that's rough," said Elizabeth.

"Poor kid—no wonder he's acting out," said La Shana. "He needs more attention than he's getting, so he's willing to settle for the negative kind. I've seen that a lot with kids who are brought in to the sheriff's office."

"How do you know all this, Cathy?" Gigi asked.

"From Mrs. Stuart," Mary Grace interjected. "It turns out, she and my grandma talk *a lot*.

"Wow. That kid has had it rough," Elizabeth stated sympathetically.

"When Grandma told me all this stuff—and I told Penelope—we both decided we feel sorry for Justin, even though he did some pretty bad stuff to us."

"That's because you are kind, empathetic girls," said La Shana. "I feel sorry for him too. He acts tough, but he looked pretty scared in that meeting on Tuesday—close to tears, even. Poor kid."

"They've already punished him with suspension," Penelope chimed in, "and now they're going to make him change classrooms in the middle of the year. Doesn't that seem a little *too* mean?"

"Kids will talk. It will be embarrassing for him," said Elizabeth.

"This may scar him for a long time. It may make him angrier than he already is," Grandma Cathy said.

"I know rules are rules," said Mrs. Li, "but perhaps these particular rules are a bit harsh for a little fifth-grader with no mom or grandma to set him straight."

"This whole thing makes me think about the 7-Eleven burglars," Mary Grace said. "Remember how you guys made sure that they understood how wrong it was to steal those things—and that they had to apologize and make up for what they did? But you also made sure that *their* problems were solved."

"Kevin and Dolly are really just so sweet," La Shana said, smiling.

"Yes," said Elizabeth, "and so much happier now that they get some company and treats when they want them."

"Well, I think this is the same kind of situation," said Mary Grace. "We need to get Mrs. Stuart to be a little nicer to Justin, now that he's finished his suspension."

"And he probably got in big trouble at home too," added Penelope. "His dad looked pretty mad at him."

"I practiced law for a long time, and I believe in laws," Grandma Cathy said, "but sometimes a punishment can be too harsh—or too lenient."

"I know what you mean," said La Shana. "I believe in the old saying, 'The punishment should fit the crime.'" La Shana's years in law enforcement had shaped her thoughts.

"Maybe Justin should have to work with the kids in Classroom Five, just like Tiffany," suggested Penelope. "It

DONNY AND MARY GRACE'S CALIFORNIA ADVENTURES

might help him understand kids like Donny better. I doubt he'd call them awful names once he got to know them."

"Good. That's a good lesson. Justin is so young; it would be nice to see something good come out of this." Everyone nodded at Mrs. Li's hopeful thought.

"You know what," Grandma Cathy announced, "we need to make a list of constructive ideas for Justin's punishment—things that might be better and more positive than making him transfer to a new classroom. I can take our list to Mrs. Stuart tomorrow, before it is too late." She took one of the pads they usually used for bridge, and started writing. "First of all . . . he could work with the kids from Classroom Five. What else?"

Grandma Cathy got out a pen and a legal pad and started writing.

"Okay, no transfer to a new classroom . . . stay in Ms. Root's class." She read out loud as she wrote, "Next, work with kids from Classroom Five."

"What else?" she asked.

"Maybe he should see a counselor," La Shana offered. "He does seem to have a problem with anger, and could certainly use somebody to talk to about that and about his situation at home."

"Good," Grandma Cathy said, and wrote down, 'See counselor.' "What else?"

"He should write apology letters, like Tiffany did—to both of us, and to Tiffany too," Mary Grace said.

"Yes, of course," said Grandma Cathy, and wrote it down. "That will encourage him to think and reflect on what he did to each of you. What else?"

"He should probably write an apology letter to Grandma Cathy and Papa Steve too, for what he said about Donny," said Mary Grace, who was always thinking of her little brother.

"And maybe even Ms. Root," chimed in Penelope.

"Whoa. This is turning into a major writing assignment," said Grandma Cathy. "But I suppose it would be good for Justin. He would certainly learn more from writing apology notes than from cleaning classrooms."

Grandma Cathy wrote down all the names that had been suggested.

"I have an idea," said Elizabeth. "I could offer Justin free karate lessons."

"That isn't exactly a punishment," said Mary Grace, laughing. "That sounds like fun!"

"Yes," said Elizabeth, "but karate teaches discipline, which is just what Justin needs. And maybe it will help him channel some of that anger—and give him something to do after school other than getting into trouble."

The others nodded, and Grandma Cathy wrote down that idea next to all the rest.

"You know," Elizabeth continued, "sometimes bullies and troublemakers are just kids who lack self-confidence. They are afraid others will hurt them, so they lash out first. I teach my students that karate is a defensive art to be used only when someone is attacking. If Mrs. Stuart is open to this idea, I can call Justin's father and tell him Justin may have four free lessons at my studio."

"Okay," said Grandma Cathy, "I think we have a pretty good list here—some creative and fair punishments—and some free karate lessons too! Now I just have to get Mrs. Stuart and Ms. Root to see it our way."

Everyone was pleased with the result of the conversation—Mary Grace, most of all. Talking things out with the Grandma Gang had been one of her best ideas yet. She was happy she'd introduced her new best friend to these strong and kind women.

CHAPTER

SEVENTEEN

T he next day, Grandma Cathy met with Mrs. Stuart, and
she agreed to all of the ideas they'd come up with.

"I like the way Mary Grace thinks," she said after
Grandma Cathy had explained the reasons behind each of
their suggestions. "That young girl has a good mind and a
big heart."

Friday night in California was Saturday morning in Africa—
and time for a family Zoom video call. There had been lots
of glitches and disconnections during previous calls, but the
internet connection was surprisingly good on this particular
evening.

After about thirty minutes of fun-filled chatter among the four people squished together on one screen and two people squished together on the other, Papa Steve said, "Okay, Donny, I think it's time for you and me to put on our pajamas and read *Green Eggs and Ham.* Say good night to your mom and dad. I'm sure we'll be talking to them again over the weekend. Bye, Jen. Bye, John. Love you guys."

"Does Papa like *Green Eggs and Ham,* Donny?" Mr. Miller asked.

"It's his favorite book now, Dad! He told me so."

"Of course it is," said Mr. Miller. "Good night, buddy! Sleep tight. Don't let the bed bugs bite."

"Good night, Daddy. They don't bite me because I don't taste very good, remember?"

"Good night, my sweet boy," said Mrs. Miller. Have sweet dreams."

"I'm gonna dream about marbles! Next time, I'll show you my cool lucky-number-eight one that Mrs. Li gave me! Good night, Mommy." Donny leaned over and kissed the computer screen, then stepped back and saw one big set of lips kiss the screen, then another.

"I got both of them," he giggled. "They were wet!"

Once Papa Steve and Donny had left the room, Mrs. Miller said, "Donny seems so happy, and so do you, Mary Grace, which makes *me* very happy too."

"Well, she *is* happy," interjected Grandma Cathy. "Mary Grace is happy to have gotten through the last couple of weeks. You should be very proud of your daughter."

And then, for the first time, Mary Grace told her parents about the bullying incident.

Justin returned to school on Monday, and was relieved to find that his classmates thought he had been out sick. Over the weekend, Mrs. Stuart had spoken with him about what he'd have to do when he got back. This included writing the apology notes Mary Grace, Penelope, and the Grandma Gang had suggested, as well as working with the kids in Classroom Five. When she told him he wouldn't have to switch to the other fifth-grade classroom, he yelped with joy and thanked her. And, of course, he was equally happy that he wouldn't have to spend his after-school time cleaning classrooms.

Mrs. Stuart had asked him to stop by her office on Monday afternoon, after the final bell, and when he arrived, she smiled and asked, "How are you feeling, Justin? You were out sick, right?" They both laughed at her little joke, but then she got serious. "Really, I'd like to know how it feels to be back at school."

"It seems like nothing ever happened," Justin responded with a shrug.

"I'm sure that is a big relief," said Mrs. Stuart, "and you have Mary Grace to thank for it. That is the way she wanted it to be."

Mrs. Stuart then had a long talk with Justin. She wanted to make it clear to him that the additional precautions and punishments that were proposed by the school board would have been much harsher and much more embarrassing. She wanted him to know that it was Mary Grace who'd suggested that he stay in Ms. Root's class. She wanted him to know that it was Mary Grace who'd argued against his detention. She wanted him to know that it was Mary Grace who had wanted to keep the entire incident private and confidential. She wanted him to know that it was Mary Grace who he had to thank for *everything*.

"That young girl wants something good to come of all this," Mrs. Stuart said, "and she has worked hard to make sure that's the case."

When Justin left Mrs. Stuart's office, he went straight to Elizabeth's studio for his first karate lesson. He loved every minute of it, and Elizabeth noted the smile on his face, even when they were doing the most challenging exercises.

When the lesson ended and the kids were getting ready to leave, Elizabeth approached her newest student.

"You know, Justin, you really catch on quick. You could be really good at this—I can tell. I want you to know that after your four free lessons are done, if you want to continue, we can work something out. Maybe you could help me clean the studio in exchange for more classes. How does that sound to you?"

"Wow. Really?!"

"Yes, really."

Justin didn't even know what to say. He was not used to people being so nice to him.

"I want to tell you something," Elizabeth said. "It takes many, many years to become a black belt in karate, but from what I have seen today, if you put in the effort, you can get there. In fact, I think you can do anything you set your mind to."

Justin's eyes grew wide. Nobody had ever said anything like that to him.

The next day, Ms. Root talked to the class about community service—volunteer work that makes the world a better place for others.

Once they understood the basics, she said, "I've written all of your names on slips of paper, and I'm going to pick two of those names out of this hat. The two names I pick will be the first to receive their community service assignments.

And . . . the first student is . . . Tiffany Johnson. The second student is . . . Justin Green."

Of course, she had been pretending. Both Tiffany and Justin knew that they would be helping Mrs. Hagen, but they didn't want anyone to wonder why—so they acted surprised when their names were called.

"You two are very lucky," continued Ms. Root, because the first community service project is a fun one. Tiffany, you will be helping Mrs. Hagen and her students at recess each day, and Justin, you will be helping her get the kids ready to leave after the final bell, and helping her organize Classroom Five for the next morning. I'm sure both Mrs. Hagen and her wonderful class will be very grateful for your presence—and I think you are really going to enjoy working with them."

Thanks to Ms. Root's great acting skills, Justin and Tiffany's secret was safe; nobody would ever find out about the notes, the suspensions, or the punishment. That made the two of them very happy. It made Mary Grace and Penelope happy too.

A couple of months later, as spring approached, Mary Grace stood by and watched as Donny ran up to Justin during recess and gave him a big high five.

"Hey, Donny," Justin said with a big smile, "I've got another marble for you today."

"Another marble? Yesss!" Marbles always made Donny happy.

Justin reached into his pocket and handed Donny a marble with a bright-blue-and-red swirling pattern.

"Wow, cool. I don't have one like this—thanks!" Donny gave Justin a big hug.

Once Justin had found out how much Donny liked marbles, he had gone through his drawers and closet to find all of the ones he'd collected when he was Donny's age. It would probably take Justin well over a year to give Donny all of them—and that was exactly what he intended to do. He was glad he'd decided to give his marbles to Donny one at a time, because he genuinely enjoyed the big hugs he got in return.

As Justin kneeled down to talk with Donny, Mary Grace looked on with a big smile on her face.

That weekend, Grandma Cathy and Papa Steve decided it was time to take another trip to the Santa Barbara Zoo to see Lucky the Penguin.

"Why don't you each bring a friend along?" Grandma Cathy suggested to her grandchildren.

"Can I bring *two?*" asked Mary Grace. "I want to bring Penelope and Tiffany."

"Sure, sweetheart," said her grandma.

"The more the merrier," said Papa Steve. "We can take the Suburban."

"I'm glad to see that the three of you girls are getting along now," said Grandma Cathy.

"Yeah, me too," replied Mary Grace. "Tiffany is trying hard to be nice to us and not be jealous. A trip to the zoo together might make things even better." Mary Grace had a great way of looking at things.

"Can I bring Justin?" asked Donny.

Grandma Cathy's eyebrows turned downward in the middle.

"Don't you have a friend from your class that you would like to bring, Donny?"

"I want Justin."

"Hmmm . . . we'll see," was all Grandma Cathy could think to say next.

"Grandma, I think bringing Justin is a great idea," said Mary Grace. "He and Donny are good friends now. Isn't that right, Donny?"

"We play every day at recess," Donny said, "and Justin brings me marbles."

"How about Ed?" suggested Grandma Cathy.

"Okay, Ed can come too!" said Donny, beaming.

That is *not* what his grandmother had had in mind, but in the end, Grandma Cathy and Papa Steve stuffed six excited kids into the back of their Suburban for a fun-filled ride to the zoo. This would be a big group to keep track of, and they were both still a bit worried about the group dynamics—*and* being responsible for six individuals when they were no longer trapped in the back of a vehicle. But they had agreed with Mary Grace that it could turn out to be a positive experience for everyone involved—and everything would probably work out just fine.

It turned out to be a wonderful and memorable day. Both Tiffany and Justin were polite, helpful, and genuinely grateful to be included. And, much to the surprise of Grandma Cathy and Papa Steve, nobody wandered off, got lost, or got in trouble. Everyone had a great time, but happiest of all was Mary Grace. They'd never seen her so happy.

When they finally got to the penguin exhibit, Mary Grace handed her phone to Grandma Cathy and asked her to take a picture of all of them standing near the *Lucky the Penguin* sign. They all posed and giggled and made faces, and Grandma Cathy snapped shot after shot until Mary Grace was satisfied that they all looked perfect. Then she texted the picture to her parents with a simple message:

So "Lucky" to be in California!

AFTERWORD

Dear reader, it's important to note that unfortunately, due to ongoing medical issues, Lucky the Penguin passed away at the Santa Barbara Zoo in 2020. The zoo continues to celebrate Lucky's life, and should you visit, you can find photos of Lucky throughout the penguin exhibit.

You can also watch videos of Lucky walking with his special boot on YouTube. He was very special, and it is easy to admire his resiliency and character . . . just like our Donny!

To learn more about The Grandma Gang, including the next book in the series, visit www.grandmagangmysteries.com.

CPSIA information can be obtained
at www.ICGtesting.com
Printed in the USA
LVHW040528230322
714082LV00013B/398/J

9 781956 470260